Guarding the Teacher

A Lesbian Paranormal Romantic Comedy

Reba Bale

GUARDING THE TEACHER

Cover by Paper or Pixels

Contents

About This Book

The agents of Sapphic Security are about to take on their most difficult challenge yet – kindergarten!

Lucy

As a teacher, I'm a mandatory reporter so when I saw the bruises on one of my students, I immediately called Child Protective Services. Now the student and his mother are in hiding and there's an angry crime boss who blames me for him losing his family. When my CEO father insists on hiring me a bodyguard, they send the most stunning woman that I've ever seen. Too bad she's so grumpy and serious.

Bella

Yeah, that's right, I'm a vampire named Bella. Cue the movie jokes. As one of the newest agents at Sapphic Security, I'm trying my best to follow all the rules. But being assigned to guard a sunshine personality kindergarten teacher while being surrounded by little kids with sticky hands all day is not exactly what I signed up for. Then I realize that Lucy is my fated mate and I'm suddenly laser focused on my mission. I need to keep her safe so I can make her mine, no matter how different we are.

I'm going to have to get creative to catch the bad guy and get the girl. Looks like I'm going to need to call in the bear shifters to help...

"Guarding the Teacher" is opposites attract instalove paranormal romantic comedy. This fun and lighthearted lesbian romance includes strong women, supernatural matchmakers, a touch of adventure, and a steamy but sweet happily ever after.

About the Sapphic Security series: They served their country as part of an elite force of supernatural soldiers. When their time in the military ends, these lesbians create Sapphic Security, providing protective and investigation services to those in need. They're fit, they're funny, and they're...va mpires. And shifters too. There's only one rule: don't fall in love with the clients. Oops. They really need to change that rule, because these sexy women are finally finding love with their fated mates.

Be sure to check out a free preview of Reba Bale's lesbian romance "The Divorcee's First Time" at the end of this book!

Join Reba Bale's Newsletter

Want a free book? Join my weekly newsletter and you'll receive a fun subscriber gift. I promise I will only email you when there are new releases, free books, or special sales you'll want to see.

Visit my newsletter sign-up page at https://books.rebabale.com/lesbianromance to join today.

Dedication

For all the teachers, and the vampires who love them.

Prologue -- Lucy

I was walking to the teacher's parking lot when I heard heavy footsteps behind me. The fine hairs on the back of my neck prickled with a sense that I was in danger as I resisted the sudden urge to run. Instead I looked over my shoulder, hoping it was one of my coworkers.

This was not my lucky day. Somehow I wasn't surprised.

Two guys the size of linebackers were walking behind me, their carefully blank faces somehow making them look more menacing. They were dressed all in black – black boots, black jeans, black tee shirts – and with their dark hair super short, I'd be hard pressed to identify either of them in a line-up. That was probably the idea.

I knew instinctively that these were Liam McMurphy's guys. Until about a week ago I had no idea that we even had the mafia here in Seattle, let alone an Irish mafia, but my eyes had been opened to a lot of things lately.

Maybe it was foolhardy of me, but there was no way I was going to cower in front of these guys. Bullies wanted you to be weak, but my father had taught me to be a strong woman. If these guys were going to do something to me, they could damn well look me in the eye while doing it. And I wasn't going to make it easy for them either.

I swung around to face them, planting my feet wide and putting my fists on my hips to make myself look bigger. I caught a flash of surprise before the thugs smoothed their expressions again.

"Why are you following me?" I demanded.

"You have something we want," one guy said smoothly, as if I'd accidentally grabbed his bag at the grocery store or had his mail misdelivered to my house.

I raised one eyebrow and waited, making him say it.

"Our boss wants his son back," the guy who'd spoken before continued. "The wife too, although if he has to make a choice, he'll take the boy."

I worked hard to keep my face blank, to give nothing away. I had a feeling that McMurphy would eventually trace his family's disappearance to me.

"I don't have them," I said. "I'm a teacher, not a kidnapper."

"You know where they are," the man said.

"I do not know where they are," I said firmly.

It was technically true. I didn't know exactly where they were, although I had a good idea. I was pretty sure that the domestic violence agency had stashed Robbie and his mom Suan at one of their hidden shelter locations around the city, although given Liam McMurphy's reach, they might have transported them out of the state just to be safe.

The goons just stared at me with their cold, dead eyes, as if the weight of their gaze would shake loose more information. When it didn't, one of them grabbed me by the shoulders, moving so quickly that it didn't even register until I felt the bite of beefy fingers squeezing through my shirt. My knee shot up out of instinct, but he blocked me with a look that bordered on condescending. So much for those self-defense classes my father had insisted on me taking. I clearly needed a refresher.

"We're going to give you a day to think about how dangerous it is to make enemies," he said in a low voice. "Especially enemies like Liam McMurphy. Next time we won't be so nice."

He flung me away from him and I went flying into the side of my car, hitting with a thump that made my teeth rattle. I stayed where I was, watching them stroll away before I finally opened the car and got inside. My hands were shaking as I tried to get the key in the ignition. I'd seen enough movies to know that these guys were not going to give up easily.

I needed help. It was time to visit my father.

Bella

I trudged into our staff meeting right behind my coworkers Angie and Teresa. Their heads were together as Teresa talked about their efforts to find a surrogate so she and her mate could have a baby.

I felt an unexpected sense of wistfulness as I eavesdropped on their conversation. I'd never thought much about finding a mate, but lately with all my coworkers getting paired up it was definitely on my mind. I hadn't exactly had good relationship role models growing up, but with the happy band of misfits who worked here at Sapphic Security, I'd have plenty of people to go to for help. If I ever found my mate that is. Not everyone was so lucky.

"Pavlovski!" I jumped as my boss Lois practically shouted my name across the conference room table. Lois had two volumes: menacing whisper and angry shout.

"Yes ma'am?"

My inner vampire bristled a little at my deference to the giant butch wolf shifter, but I'd spent enough years in the Army to learn to have respect for my senior officers. Besides, Lois was twice my size. She could snap me like a twig.

"I have an assignment for you."

I opened my notebook and picked up my pen to take notes. "What do we have?"

"Kindergarten teacher got on the wrong side of the mob when she helped someone go into hiding."

"Someone?" I asked.

"This particular mob boss is a wife beater."

Lois practically spat out the words. She hated people who preyed on those who were weaker.

"When he put his hands on the kid too, the teacher noticed and decided to help them get away. The guy is very interested in locating his family, and not afraid to shake down the teacher to make it happen."

"What's the plan?" I asked.

"You're going undercover. You will be the new kindergarten educational aid."

"I don't even know what that is," I said.

"It was the client's idea," Lois said impatiently. "She'll explain it all. It's like a classroom helper or something. I think you're gonna hand out fingerpaints and shit. Help keep kids from escaping. Change diapers. Whatever it is they do in kindergarten."

I groaned internally. I'd never changed a diaper in my life.

"Kindergarten is where they teach kids to read and write," Angie piped up helpfully. "They learn socialization and numbers and how to use scissors, that kind of thing. They're already potty trained before they start."

"Maybe you should take this assignment," I mumbled. "You seem to know a lot about it."

Kindergarten sounded boring as fuck. Plus I wasn't really a kid person. I hadn't been around kids since I was one, other than my little sister. And she was born self-sufficient.

"No can do," Angie said cheerfully, clearly amused at my lack of enthusiasm. "I'm already busy with other projects."

"No switching assignments," Lois barked, making me jump. "This isn't a damned democracy."

Lois ran her hand over her buzz cut, a nervous tic that told me she was reaching for her patience. It didn't take much. My boss only had patience for one person: her mate.

"Who's my partner?" I asked.

We usually did personal security assignments in teams, partly because two sets of eyes were better than one, and partly because none of us could be awake twenty-four seven.

"You're going in alone."

My head shot up in surprise.

"Everyone else is on assignment – or on a damned honeymoon or something," Lois explained with an annoyed look. "You'll go in, get the lay of the land, and set up a plan. If things are more complicated than you can handle, we'll see if we can pull in one of the bears."

The 'bears' were Belarusian bear shifter brothers who had served in the military in their home country before becoming CIA operatives and moving to the United States. They were semi-retired and running a restaurant here in Seattle but still took contract work for Sapphic Security and some of the more clandestine government agencies.

I didn't know the bears as well as some of my teammates – I was the newest agent here – but I'd only heard good things about working with them. Plus they could all cook, which was more than I could say.

"Got it, boss."

Lois slid a folder of information across the table to me. "You'll meet the client at the school after this meeting."

Two hours later I parked my car in the teacher's lot at New Day Elementary School. From my research I'd learned it was a private school for Seattle's wealthier residents, those who wouldn't deign to send their kids to public school like the rest of us.

I scanned the parking lot, noting that the cars got fancier the closer I got to the building. Presumably, that was where the administration parked. The building itself was one level, a sprawling brick facade surrounded by perfectly manicured grass and beds full of flowers and decorative bushes.

It was a far cry from the cement box where I went to grade school.

After being buzzed in, a very tiny elderly woman wearing a sweater set and pearls led me down one of the long hallways that branched off from the administration offices.

“Lucy must be thrilled,” the woman, who told me her name was Ethel, said as she marched me down the hallway at a surprisingly fast clip, given her age and size. “She hasn’t had a classroom aid all year. Fortunately, you’re here right between sessions so you two will have a chance to talk before the kids start coming back in.”

“Great,” I mumbled, figuring she was expecting an answer.

I hadn’t gone home to change before coming over here and based on the look that Ethel gave me, my attire wasn’t totally suitable for the job. Then again, all of my clothes were essentially the same: dark pants, black boots, dark colored shirts, and during the cooler months, my favorite black leather jacket. I probably looked more like a biker chick than a kindergarten teacher’s helper.

As we walked down the hallway my vampire side started getting agitated. She wasn't very verbal in general, communicating mostly in pictures and feelings, but it was clear she was riled up about something. I swiveled my head from side to side, trying to figure out what my vamp was focused on.

There. It was a scent. A mixture of something sweet, like a tropical flower, and something that was reminiscent of coconut. As we walked down the hallway the scent was getting stronger and stronger, making my vamp even more excited. I didn't sense any danger though, just interest.

Ethel stopped in front of a door at the very end of the hallway.

"Here we are."

She gave a perfunctory knock, then pushed the door open, calling out, "Lucy, your new educational aid is here."

I stepped inside, my eyes doing a cursory sweep of the room out of habit before focusing on the woman walking towards me. She was a human, small and soft, with pale white skin, straight hair that was somewhere between blonde and brown, and huge brown eyes. She was dressed more professionally than I expected for a kindergarten teacher, in tan khakis that molded to her round hips, black Keds, a black scoop necked shirt, and a grey and black blazer.

She gave me a crooked smile that seemed full of mischief despite the serious situation she was facing.

"Bella? Hi, I'm Lucy, it's so nice to meet you."

When she stuck out her hand I engulfed her fingers in mine, and I heard her inhale softly as a little hum of electricity traveled between our skin. My vamp spoke one single word: *mine!* My eyes flew to Lucy's and that's when I knew the truth: I'd finally found my fated mate.

I just wasn't sure I was happy about it. A fragile human? A sweet little kindergarten teacher? This was my fated mate? Surely there had been some kind of mistake.

My vampire rumbled deep inside me. *Not a mistake. Mate.*

Lucy

The woman in front of me was examining me like I was a puzzle she couldn't figure out. Maybe it was a bodyguard thing, or maybe that was how she always was, I had no idea.

Bella was stunning. Wavy blonde hair and dark clothes gave her a little bit of a rocker chick vibe. She was slim but muscled, with smallish breasts and narrow hips, but a hint of softness that appealed to me. She wasn't the kind of woman I was typically attracted to, but as soon as she touched me, my core started tingling in a way it hadn't done in a very long time.

Bella's blue eyes scanned the room before returning to my face, never letting go of my hand the entire time.

She radiated power. I was sure she was ex-military – my father told me that all the agents at Sapphic Security were – but there was something else. It reminded me of my friend and fellow teacher Elena who was a shape shifter. I'd known since I was a child that shifters and other magical creatures lived alongside us in the human world, but I hadn't spent a lot of time with non-humans until Elena and I became friends. At least not to my knowledge. I knew that the supernatural crowd tried hard to fly under the radar so the humans wouldn't mess with them.

Maybe Bella was a shifter. That would explain what seemed different about her. She wasn't a bear shifter, that was obvious. She was too slim for that. I'd met most of Elena's family and they were all big boned and tall. Bella was lithe and all coiled power, like a jaguar or something. Maybe a tiger.

I wondered if it was rude to ask her. Although Elena could probably figure it out. She told me before she could identify most shifters by scent.

"I'm going to get back to the office now."

Ethel's curious voice broke the spell between us. Damn it, I was so distracted by my bodyguard I totally forgot the school secretary was even there. I dropped Bella's hand like it was on fire, resisting the urge to rub it on my pants.

"You girls let me know if you need anything."

"Thanks Ethel."

Once my coworker had left, Bella went into business mode.

"I need to know everything about what's happening to you," she demanded. "Don't leave anything out."

I shook my head. "It will have to wait. The kids will be coming in ten minutes, and I need to brief you on what we're doing this afternoon. If they smell fear, those kids will eat you alive."

Bella's spine snapped even straighter than it had already been. She was a prickly one.

"I'm not afraid of a bunch of five year olds."

"Then you're foolish," I said lightly. "They're little monsters. Let me show you around. Do you have any experience in education or childcare?"

"No."

"Babysitting?"

"No."

"I was hoping they could send someone who at least knew something about kids," I sighed.

"Would you rather have someone who can protect you or someone who can play pattycakes?" she snapped.

I couldn't help the snort that escaped from my nose. "You really know nothing about children."

As I reviewed the afternoon plan with Bella my mind was preoccupied on the conversation I'd had with my parents last night. I didn't often go to them for help – in fact I never went to them for help – but I knew I was out over my skis with this Liam McMurphy thing. So I'd driven out to my parents' giant house on Lake Washington and dumped the whole story on them.

By the time I was finished my father was texting the head of his security detail looking for options. As the CEO of one of the country's largest airplane manufacturing companies, my Dad had security full-time. Mom too. There were a lot of crazies out there eager to kidnap or kill someone with the kind of money and prestige that Dad had.

He'd had security on me when I was a kid but once I graduated college I insisted that he let them go. I couldn't live my life with burly guys following me all the time, whispering into their Bluetooth headphones. Besides, I'd stayed out of the spotlight my entire life and my parents had been very careful to never allow a picture of me or anything about me to be published in the press or on the internet. Most people didn't know that Lucy Ingram was any relation to Robert Ingram, and that's the way we all liked it.

I'd asked Dad to try to get me a female bodyguard, which was how we ended up with Bella. Apparently Sapphic Security's entire staff was female-identified, ex-military, and presumably sapphic, based on the name. A terrifying woman named Lois came to the house an hour later, explaining that she was the director of our local Sapphic Security office, part of a larger company with offices around the globe. After asking me a few questions, we came up with a plan for my protection agent to pose as my educational aid.

An agent would also stay with me at my house overnight, although I wasn't sure if it was going to be Bella or someone else.

A bell in the corridor interrupted my musing. Bella jumped, then spun around, pulling me behind her like she'd heard gunfire.

"Relax, it's the bell," I said, slipping around her. "The kids are coming back from lunch. We do a full day kindergarten here."

Less than thirty seconds later the door flew open, and twenty kids came racing inside the room. They were always particularly energetic after they ate lunch even though the school served an organic, mostly sugar free lunch.

I clapped my hands to get their attention, and every child froze where they were.

"Who had a nice lunch?" I called, holding up my hand.

Twenty hands shot up.

"What do we do after lunch?" I asked. "Who can tell me?"

"Letters," about five kids called out at the same time.

"Yes, nice job, but before we work on letters, who wants to meet my new friend?"

Twenty hands flew up in the air again and I suppressed a smile.

"Everyone, this is Miss Bella. She is going to be my special helper in the classroom. Say hello to Miss Bella."

"Hello Miss Bella," the kids spoke as one.

Bella was staring at them like they all had bombs strapped to their chests.

"Smile," I whispered out of the side of my mouth. "Look friendly."

Bella moved her face into something I think was supposed to be a smile, but it looked more like a grimace. I rolled my lips in to keep from laughing.

"Let's get to know Miss Bella so she can be your new friend too," I called. "Everyone please sit at your desk and put on your listening ears."

I tweaked both of my ears with my fingers and the kids moved into their tiny chairs and followed suit. "Now who has a question for Miss Bella?"

"Are you married?" one kid called.

I wanted to know that myself.

"No," she said shortly.

"Do you have a dog?" another kid asked.

Bella shook her head.

"Do you have a cat? A bird? A baby?" the questions came at her rapid fire from around the room.

"I do not have any living thing in my apartment besides myself," Bella said seriously.

"But where are your mommy and daddy?" one girl asked in obvious concern.

Bella shot me a look before answering, "They live... somewhere else."

Having a feeling that we shouldn't explore that any further, I asked, "Do you at least have a plant at your house?"

"No."

"Well, that's super sad, isn't it, class?" I asked, making an exaggerated sad face.

The kids all mimicked me.

"How about today we work on the letter P and then we can draw Miss Bella some pictures of plants for her apartment?"

The kids cheered like I'd just given them a million bucks.

And that was what I liked about teaching kindergarten.

"Miss Bella will help pass out crayons," I said, handing her a plastic bin full of boxes of crayons.

Bella shrugged off her leather jacket, setting it on a shelf near the window, then went from desk to desk handing out crayons. I handed out drawing paper, aware that my bodyguard watched me carefully. God, she was sexy. I had a sudden urge to throw her down on my desk and have my way with her.

Bella looked at me over her shoulder and I had the strangest feeling that she knew exactly what I was thinking. And then she gave me a sexy smirk that confirmed it. I resisted the urge to fan myself. Wow.

Bella

I hadn't really been around kids before, but even I could tell that Lucy was good with them. Most of them paid close attention to everything she said, and the ones who didn't Lucy quickly put back on track. She was warm but held boundaries.

She'll make a good mother to our children, my vamp said helpfully.

I walked around distributing crayons and offering encouragement for the plant pictures the kids were drawing, keeping my awareness on my mate. Sure, it was my job as her bodyguard, but even if it wasn't, my inner vampire wouldn't allow me to do anything else. She was restless inside me, excited about finding a mate, pressing me to mark her.

We don't even know if she knows about vampires, I reminded us both.

It was probably strange to humans, talking to a part of yourself that was separate and sentient, but for those of us who grew up in the dual-natured magical world, it was normal. We'd learned as kids not to speak out loud to our other halves, at least not unless we were alone, lest the humans think we were mentally ill.

Technically, the fact that shifters and vampires and fae and witches lived and walked amongst the humans wasn't a secret, but most humans remained oblivious. Our people had agreed long ago that if we kept our magical sides mostly hidden the humans wouldn't bother us.

I felt the weight of Lucy's gaze. She appeared to be looking down at something on her desk, but her eyes were lifted, watching me through her eyelashes. She'd felt something when we touched, and I could sense that she was as attracted to me as I was to her. Of course she had no idea it was the mate bond – she probably didn't even know what mates were – but I'd seen the way she'd stared at where our hands were joined, a little crinkle between her eyebrows like something didn't compute.

I wasn't sure what the protocol was here. Should I tell her that she was my mate? Should I report it to my boss Lois? And if I did, would she pull me off this job? My fangs pressed against my lips as I thought about one of my coworkers guarding my mate instead of me. They were mostly all mated, but there was no way I was taking a chance. No, the best plan was probably just to stay in bodyguard mode until the danger had passed then I'd ask Lucy out on a date. Court her like a human. Then eventually I could break the news about the vampire thing.

Little did I know I wasn't going to have that chance.

It was a few hours later and all the children had been picked up by their parents, leaving an almost unnatural silence in the room. I was woman enough to admit that after hours of constant questions, high pitched screams, whining, and trying to keep the kids focused, I was freaking exhausted.

Suddenly the door swung open while I was helping Lucy clean up the classroom so we could get out of here. Without a conscious thought, I jumped in front of her, ready to protect her from whoever was coming in.

"Lucy, I...uh..."

A woman stood in the doorway, looking at me with open suspicion. She was tall – at least an inch or two over six feet – and what my mother would have called 'stocky'. Not fat, just solid and muscled. Her golden brown hair fell down her back in soft waves, and I could see the animal flickering behind her eyes. I sniffed subtly. Bear.

"Vampire," the woman sneered. As a rule, vamps and shifters weren't very fond of each other. "What are you doing in here?"

Before I could answer she stalked forward to look over my shoulder. The woman was tall enough to do it, which made my inner vamp bristle.

"Are you okay, Lucy? Did she hurt you?"

I couldn't help the hiss that escaped my mouth at the intimation that I would hurt my mate. My eyes locked on the bear, who glared back at me menacingly, growling low in her throat.

Lucy stepped out from behind me and looked between us.

"What's happening right now?" she asked. "Why do you look like you're about to fight?"

When we didn't answer, Lucy's voice turned bossy in a way that made my nipples harden.

"Both of you put your fangs away and step back. Now."

The bear and I obeyed immediately, something that would make me laugh later. Two alpha predators in the room and we both submitted to a curvy little kindergarten teacher.

"Why is there a vampire here?" the bear asked, turning her gaze towards Lucy. Her voice was gentler now.

"Oh, she's a vampire? I was going to ask you. I could tell she wasn't human, but I couldn't tell if she was a shifter or what."

My head snapped in Lucy's direction in surprise. "You could tell I wasn't fully human?"

"Of course." Lucy rolled her eyes. "I'm not an idiot. Bella, this is my friend and coworker Elena, she teaches the other kindergarten class. Elena, this is my bodyguard and new educational assistant, Bella."

"You're a vampire named Bella?" Elena asked with a booming laugh. "That's hilarious."

"Yeah yeah, laugh it up, Bear," I grumbled. "I've never heard that joke before."

"So anyway," Elena turned back to Lucy, clearly dismissing me. "How about getting a beer? It's been a day."

"I'll need to bring Bella," Lucy said.

"I can protect you," Elena said. "I can tear those mofos up with one swipe of my paws."

"Well maybe you and Bella can work together on that," Lucy said diplomatically. "And I'd love a beer."

Lucy looked at me. "Can you drink beer?" she asked. "Or do you have to stick with blood?"

I resisted the urge to roll my eyes. Humans were painfully uneducated about supernaturals. They believed whatever they saw in movies was true.

"I already had a shot of blood today," I told her. "That's all I usually need unless I'm injured or something. And if you're going for a beer, I'm going with you."

"Who is my night coverage?" she asked. "Maybe they want to come instead."

I frowned. "I'm your night coverage. We're a little short-handed right now, so I'm doing double duty on your protective detail. Speaking of which, I really need to hear about everything that has happened so far. It will help me plan the best way to protect you."

She patted my arm.

"We can do all that over a beer. Elena hasn't heard the whole story yet, this way I can tell you both at the same time."

The bear glared at me again as we headed for the door.

"Hold on," I said, stopping Lucy's progress. "I forgot my jacket."

After locating my jacket we took two cars to a hole-in-the-wall bar about a mile and a half away, Elena going in her car and Lucy and I driving in mine. She'd tried to insist that we take her car, but after I explained that my Sapphic Security vehicle was bullet proof and kitted out with multiple protective features, she gave in and followed me to my car. As we walked, I scanned the parking lot, looking for threats, only relaxing when we were finally in the safety of my vehicle.

Then I had another problem. Being in such close quarters with my mate was making my vampire go crazy. Her scent surrounded us, the coconut notes stronger than they'd been in the classroom. And as we traveled, another scent wafted in my direction. Arousal. I rolled my lips in, forcing my fangs to say retracted in my gums despite the way they were pressing to come out.

"What's wrong?" Lucy asked, making me startle.

"What? Nothing. Why?"

"You look different. Your skin is turning whiter, and you seem to be vibrating. Also your fingernails are getting longer, and your voice sounds rougher."

My mate was an observant little thing.

"Vamp issue, nothing to worry about," I said curtly.

When I chanced a look at her out of the side of my eye, I could tell she didn't believe me.

"What's the story with the bear?" I asked, partly to distract her.

"The bear has a name," she said firmly. "Elena has been my best friend for years."

"So you trust her?"

"Of course I trust her," Lucy replied indignantly. "Elena and I are closer than sisters. And when she heard that I'd been threatened, the first thing she did was offer to come stay with me until everything blows over."

"Why did you hire a bodyguard then?" I asked.

She sighed. "My father insisted. He said Elena wasn't trained as a bodyguard, and also that the best bodyguards are detached. Focused on their jobs. He said Elena's affection for me would distract her from protecting me fully. He's worked with your firm before and told me you were a better option."

"He's right," I agreed. "The Sapphic Security team is the best in the world. Guaranteed."

"Because you're all ex-military, or because you're all supernaturals?" she asked, and I could tell by the slight question in her tone that she wasn't sure.

"Both," I said. "Being supes gives us strength and speed and other skills that humans don't have. But being ex-military ensures that we have discipline and tactical skills. The combination makes us excellent protective agents."

"And the sapphic thing?" she asked. "How does that factor in?"

I shrugged. "Our sexual orientation has nothing to do with our ability to do the job."

"Yet it's in the name of your company."

She had a point. I'd never thought about why we were called Sapphic Security. It wasn't like everyone there was sapphic. We were mostly lesbians, bisexuals, and trans women, but we also had a few staff who were non-binary or heterosexual.

"I'll have to ask about that," I said. "I never thought about our name before."

"Turn right up here," she pointed through the windshield. "It's that place, Andy's Bar."

"Wait here," I ordered as I parked the car.

"Yes ma'am," she mumbled sarcastically.

I got out of the car and looked around, making sure everything looked okay before going around to the passenger side of the SUV and helping Lucy exit the vehicle. As we walked away, I grabbed her hand, threading her fingers through mine.

"What are you doing?" she asked, giving my hand a slight tug.

"We should pretend that we're dating when we're out in public."

It was the first thing I could come up with to explain my desire to hold her hand. Normally I wasn't a touchy feely person, but as soon as our hands locked together, my entire body relaxed a bit.

"I can't date my educational assistant," she said, tugging her hand away. I resisted the urge to growl. "It's against the rules."

It's forbidden, a voice in my head said, oddly titillated by the idea. I couldn't even blame my vamp for that. It was all me.

Lucy

I was wedged into a booth at the very back of the bar, Bella on one side and the wall on the other. Elena sat across from us, looking amused for some reason. Every few seconds Bella's eyes scanned the room, looking for danger.

I wonder how it would feel to have all that intense focus aimed at me, I thought with a tiny shiver. Bella's head snapped in my direction and for a second her nostrils flared, making me wonder if vampires had an enhanced sense of smell like the shifters did. If so, Bella was as aware as I was that my panties were turning damp from our proximity.

I really needed to date more if being pressed up against an attractive woman was enough to make me ready to climb her like a tree. I mean, the woman was just trying to do a job and here I was objectifying her.

"Tell me what happened with McMurphy," Bella ordered. "From the beginning."

Something in her tone made Elena's eyes narrow. My friend was slow to anger, but when she'd had enough her temper was explosive. Wanting to forestall whatever weirdness was going on between the two supernatural beings at the table, I started talking.

"There's a boy in my class named Robbie. He's a sweet little guy, very quiet," I began. "His mother Suan usually brought him to class and picked him up and she always seemed... off."

"How?" Bella asked.

I shrugged. "It was a sense I got. She was watchful. Nervous. Always wearing long sleeves even when it was warm out. Once the hem of her shirt got caught on a doorknob and I saw she was bruised along her side, like someone had kicked her in the ribs or something."

"I hate abusive assholes like that," Bella said, disgust thick in her tone.

"It made me start watching the boy more carefully. One day he came to class and I noticed he was walking very gingerly. Wouldn't lean back in his chair. He just seemed... different," I explained. "I was trying to decide how serious it was when he spilt his juice box on himself. I called in someone to watch my class while we went into the coat room to change Robbie's shirt. We keep extras around for situations like these and I was hoping it would give me the opportunity to see what was wrong."

I paused, taking a drink of my beer before returning.

"He, um, his back was badly bruised, and there were finger marks on one of his upper arms. I asked him about it, and Robbie began to cry. He told me that it was his fault because he'd made his father angry."

I paused as I saw the little boy's tear-streaked face in my mind.

"When his mother arrived, I sent Robbie over to play in Elena's classroom, and we talked. Suan broke down, swore she had no idea that her husband had hurt her son. She seemed so devastated that I believed her. She kept saying that she tried to protect Robbie, and that it had never happened before. Then she asked for help."

I swallowed the lump in my throat and Elena spoke up.

"As teachers we are mandatory reporters, so we had to call social services. But Lucy and I went to college with someone who runs a domestic violence program. We called in a favor, and given the involvement of the child, she agreed that social services could drop them off at one of their shelters instead of going on a waiting list," Elena said. "Given the criminal involvement of the husband, they've probably stashed her far away from Seattle, some place with strong security."

We paused as a basket of fries was delivered, Elena and I digging in immediately. I shot Bella a look.

"Vampires don't like fries?" I asked.

She gave me a look I couldn't interpret. "I don't like to put junk in my body."

"That beer you're drinking isn't exactly a health food."

Her eyes flared with heat.

I couldn't say why I felt compelled to needle her. After all, she was here to help me. But something inside me wanted to make her drop the mask so I could see the woman beneath.

Bella grabbed a handful of fries and dumped them on the small plate the server had set in front of her. "Happy now?" she asked as she picked up a fry.

Her eyes closed briefly in appreciation.

"I sure am," I said smugly. "It's a shame to waste good fries."

"What happened next?" she said sharply. "After they took away the woman and the kid?"

I told her about the threat in the parking lot last night, the specifics of which Elena hadn't heard yet. My friend made a growling noise in the back of her throat, showing her displeasure. She'd always been protective of me.

"There's one more thing," I said. "Maybe it was my imagination, but I could have sworn someone had been looking around inside my classroom when I came in this morning. Things were moved."

"Could it have been the janitor?" Bella asked.

"No. They don't go through people's desk drawers or try to log into their computers."

Without a word, Bella slid her phone out of her pocket and pressed a button. Elena and I exchanged a glance.

"Hey boss, it's Bella. I think we're going to need a second agent at the school. It's been compromised."

I heard a loud voice, but I couldn't make out the words. Whatever Bella's boss was saying, Elena could clearly hear it though.

"The other agent can fill in as my aid," Elena piped up. "Then they'll be right next door if something goes down on school grounds."

Bella gave her a nod, then said, "Sure, any of them will be good. Whoever is available. Okay, I'll call you later."

When Bella hung up Elena asked, "You have bears working there? I'm surprised I didn't know that. I know most of the bears in the area."

"Bears?" I asked in confusion.

Elena gave me a teasing look. "Puny humans with your weak ears. Bella's boss said that they were going to need to deploy one of the bears."

"They're technically contractors," Bella said, looking annoyed at Elena's eavesdropping. "They're from Belarus, I'm not surprised you don't know them."

Elena's eyebrows rose and she leaned forward to whisper, "Oh you're talking about the CIA guys? Yeah I heard they're good."

"How do you even know that?" Bella asked.

"The bear community is very tight," Elena said. "The arrival of three good-looking unmated bears was big news a couple of years ago. Why do you think their restaurant is so popular? Every bear mama is eating there, trying to find a match for their unmated daughters."

"Has your mom been there?" I asked curiously.

"Oh no, Mama gave up on me a long time ago," Elena laughed. "For a while she was hoping that you and I would get together..."

Elena was interrupted by Bella making one of those angry hissing noises again. Her fangs had dropped enough that they looked stark against the blood red color of her lips. I watched in fascination.

"Don't worry, vampire," Elena's tone was mocking now. "As much as I love your... uh, as much as I love Lucy, my bread's not buttered on that side. I like dick. The bigger the better."

Bella immediately relaxed.

We spent the next hour engaged in small talk while we finished our beer and fries. Despite Bella's initial protest, I noticed that she ate her fair share of our extra-large basket of fries. Not that I could blame her. They were delicious, perfectly crispy on the outside and soft on the inside.

"Well I'd better get home," Elena said as we finished up. "I have some laundry to do. And I'm sure you two have a lot to talk about."

I had the impression that Elena wasn't talking about personal protection, but before I could question her, she slid out of the booth, tossing a twenty on the table.

"Happy hour is on me. I'll see you tomorrow at school." She paused to give Bella a hard look. "Keep her safe."

"I intend to," Bella replied coolly.

They had a long moment of aggressive eye contact before Elena finally nodded and stepped back. "I believe you will."

Her expression softened and she gave me a fond look. "See ya tomorrow, Lucy."

As she walked away I turned to Bella. "What was all that about?"

"Nothing," Bella said.

She was lying, I could feel it, but who was I to make her talk if she didn't want to?

"When is this bear guy coming?" I asked.

"He'll meet us at school in the morning," she said. "Let's go to your place so I can make sure it's secure."

I had a thought.

"I live in a one-bedroom apartment," I said. "One of us is going to have to sleep on the couch if you're staying with me."

"I'll sleep on the floor," Bella said firmly.

"The hell you will."

She looked surprised at my response.

"No guest of mine is sleeping on the floor," I continued.

"I'm not a guest," she reminded me. "You're my client."

"That doesn't mean I can't be a good hostess."

"Let's talk about this at your place," Bella said firmly.

I rolled my eyes. "Does that bossy act work on your other clients?"

She paused as if she was considering my question. "Usually. But you're not like my other clients."

"You got that right," I confirmed as I slid out of the booth and handed Bella the jacket she'd left on the seat. "Kindergarten teachers are made of stern stuff."

Bella

I grabbed my bag from the back of the SUV and followed Lucy up to her apartment. She lived in a four story building which looked like it had been built within the last ten years or so. Seattle was full of these boxy looking new apartments, all of them looking basically the same, most of them shoehorned into small lots that used to be single family housing.

At least Lucy had an assigned parking space here. Most of these new buildings were built with little or no parking, which was making it nearly impossible to park in some neighborhoods. I pulled into her space and led Lucy inside, watching our surroundings carefully.

We were both quiet as we entered the elevator, standing as far apart as we could in the small space. Even though I was annoyed at the time, I was glad that the bear had told Lucy I was a vampire. Now I didn't have to figure out how to tell her and risk Lucy freaking out about it.

I was pretty sure Elena knew that we were fated mates. Between her knowing glances and the way she'd almost slipped when referring to Lucy, she seemed to have figured it out. I was glad she didn't blab about the mate thing, although it was basic protocol with supernaturals. If your mate was a human, it was up to you to explain all that, not someone else.

I wondered what my mother would have thought of me being with a human. Mom had died years ago, not that long after I graduated from basic training, but she'd been a big believer in supes staying with their own kind.

Not that I had a choice. Every supernatural in the world knew that fated mates were beyond our control. We didn't have to accept the gift of a mate of course, but it was painful, seriously painful, if we didn't. And worse yet, once you found your fated mate, it was impossible to be with another person who wasn't your mate. If things didn't work out with the being you were fated to be with, you were destined to spend the rest of your life alone. And celibate.

Just the word flitting through my mind made my pussy clench. I'd been in a low level of arousal since I laid eyes on Lucy, and worse yet, the bear had known. She hadn't said anything, but I knew she could smell my attraction for Lucy the same way she could smell Lucy's for me.

I had a feeling that Lucy would be mortified if she knew any of that. She was playing cool with me, but her body didn't lie. She was attracted to me. Big time. And while I didn't know much about supe/human mating, I'd heard enough from my coworkers to know that the humans felt it the same as us, even if they didn't understand what was happening.

"Hold on," I said softly as Lucy tried to exit the elevator.

I moved closer to whisper in her ear.

"Let me go first, and don't talk until I've cleared the apartment, okay?"

"Um. Okay."

I leaned out of the elevator, one hand holding onto Lucy's wrist, the other resting on the butt of the gun I'd hidden in a waist holster. Looking one way, and then the other, I determined that the hallway was clear.

“Which unit?”

“Four oh five.”

We walked to the apartment door, and I gently swung Lucy around until her back was pressed against the wall next to the door. Grabbing her keys, I opened the door, then pulled her in behind me. My skin buzzed where my fingers shackled her wrist, but I ignore that, pulling a scanning device out of my pocket to test for both explosives and recording devices.

Focusing on the task at hand, I moved slowly and methodically through her apartment. The inside was as generic as the outside, but my mate had tried to liven the place up with colorful rugs and pillows, overstuffed furniture, and plants. Lots and lots of plants, lined up along the windowsills, hanging from the ceiling, and on top of shelves and tables, an explosion of green.

No wonder she’d been so aghast earlier today when I told her that I didn’t have any plants at home. This place was practically a greenhouse.

“You like plants, huh?” I said wryly as we returned to the living room.

Lucy raised one eyebrow in question.

"We're clear," I confirmed.

"What were you checking for?" she asked.

"Listening devices. And explosives."

Her eyes widened almost comically. "You think McMurphy would *bomb* my *apartment building?*" she asked. "I'm not the only one who lives here."

"Guys like McMurphy don't care about shit like that," I said.

Lucy just stared at me in horror.

I walked to my bag, ruffling through the contents. "Do you mind if I put some stuff in your fridge?" I asked.

"Sure."

I had a small soft-sided cooler with some snacks and a couple of jars of blood. While none of it needed to be refrigerated, it all tasted better cold. Lucy's refrigerator was surprisingly empty, but I didn't comment, just stashed my stuff on one side of the bottom shelf before turning my attention back to my mate.

"Let's talk about the rules."

"Rules?" she asked.

"Yes, it's important that you know what to expect from me, and that I know what to expect from you."

Lucy sighed. "Well if we're going to do that, we're going to need a snack. I'm going to make some popcorn."

She stood up on her tiptoes to reach a box of microwave popcorn out of the cabinet. At some point she'd removed her little blazer and when she stretched, the hem of her shirt rose, revealing a strip of pale flesh. My mouth watered.

It's her waist, I told myself sternly. *There's nothing sexy about that.*

Myself disagreed.

While Lucy made a bag of popcorn, she reached into the fridge and grabbed two bottles of water, handing one to me without a word. I twisted the top off and drained half the bottle with one gulp. Lucy stared at me.

She jumped as the timer dinged, letting her know the popcorn was done. Lucy dumped it into a bowl and then brought it to the tiny kitchen table.

"Sit down," she said, pointing to the chair opposite of her.

She really was a bossy little thing.

"Okay," I said, getting down to business in an attempt to concentrate on something, anything, besides the sweet smell of my mate and how much I wanted to kiss her. "Let's talk ground rules. You don't go anywhere without me at your side. Anywhere. I need to be close to you at all times."

"What if you're in the bathroom?"

"Huh?" I stopped with a handful of popcorn halfway to my mouth. I hadn't even realized that I grabbed some.

"What if you're in the bathroom? Do I need to be at your side then?" Lucy asked with a deceptively innocent look.

"Well, no."

"What if *I'm* in the bathroom?" she pressed. "Because I have to tell you, I get terrible performance anxiety. I can't pee if I know someone else is listening."

I just stared at her for a long moment, trying to decide if she was fucking with me. With great self-control I resisted telling her that my hearing was good enough that I'd be able to hear her peeing even if she was in the next apartment.

"You don't need to take 'at my side' quite that literally," I settled on saying. "Next rule, which is really just a corollary of the first rule, don't go anywhere alone. Even just to take out the trash or grab the Uber Eats order. I don't want you exposed."

"I don't have an Uber Eats account," she answered. "I prefer Door Dash."

"Next rule, I'm trying to protect you. Quit fucking with me."

"I'm not fucking with you," she said archly. "Believe me, you'd be having way more fun if I was fucking you."

I felt a rush of arousal flood my core.

"I said fucking *with* me," I reminded her.

She shrugged. "I said what I said."

"Next rule," I said, deciding it was best to move on. "I'm going to give you a tracker disguised as a necklace. Wear it at all times."

I pulled the pouch out of my pocket and slid it across the table.

"Even in the shower?"

"It's waterproof," I assured her. "If someone snatches you, I can track you with the necklace."

"Does that happen a lot?" she asked.

"What?"

"People snatching your clients?"

"More than you'd expect," I mumbled, thinking about how a couple of our clients had gone missing until their mates had tracked them down.

"You're not instilling confidence," Lucy said.

Somehow I knew she was still teasing me even though her expression remained serious. Even still, I wanted to reassure her, so I reached across the table and took her hand in mine. Her fingers felt delicate in my palm.

"I promise that I will protect you with my life," I said, giving her a serious look. "In the unlikely event that we get separated, I will move heaven and Earth to find you and when I do, I will rip out the throat of whoever dared to even think about hurting you."

Lucy blinked, like she was surprised by the intensity of my words. To be honest, so was I.

"Would you get to drink their blood?"

"What?"

"Y'all have a rule you can't drink blood from humans without their consent right? But if you've killed them while defending someone, is that blood up for grabs?"

I just stared at her for a long moment.

"I'll have to look that up in the vampire handbook," I finally said.

The truth was, I could, but I didn't want to put that visual in my mate's mind.

Lucy smirked. "Do that, because I really want to know."

Lucy

Normally I was a pretty serious person. I mean, I could have fun. I liked to laugh. But as a rule, my default was serious. Except with Bella. For some reason I felt this urge to mess with her. To tease some of her own seriousness away. I was dying to see her smile. A real smile, not that fake grimace smile she gave the kids.

Someday I was going to get her to smile, but it wasn't going to be today.

After we'd discussed everything we needed to discuss, I suggested that we watch a movie.

"Just do whatever you would normally do," Bella told me. "I'll be here."

Her answer was weird.

"Here doing what?" I asked.

She frowned. "Working. Making sure you're okay."

"I'd rather you watched a movie with me."

"I don't watch a lot of movies," Bella said.

"Great, then whatever we pick will be new to you. Let me just change my clothes."

I stopped in the bathroom to wash up and use the facilities, then I changed into flannel sleep pants, socks, and a sweatshirt without a bra. My normal sleep attire. It wasn't sexy. But then again I'd been sleeping alone for way longer than I wanted to admit. And as attracted to Bella as I was, I wasn't trying to make myself sexy for her.

She was here to do a job. I understood that. This wasn't going to be like one of those romantic bodyguard movies where the bodyguard and client fall in love and live happily ever after once the credits roll. I was pragmatic enough to know that I was just a client to Bella, and when she was done with me, she'd move onto the next person who needed her.

She was attracted to me though, I could tell that instinctively although I wasn't sure how. I was tempted to suggest a little sexual release, but even after knowing Bella for less than a day I could tell she'd never break the rules like that. And I knew without checking that sleeping with a client would definitely be against the rules at Sapphic Security. I didn't want to get her in trouble just because I was horny.

Dropping on one end of the couch, I pulled my knees up to my chest and grabbed the remote.

"What do you want to watch?" I asked.

Bella came over to join me on the couch, sitting on the other side, leaving a cushion between us.

"Whatever you want."

"What do you like?" I pressed. "Romantic comedies? Superheroes? Tearjerkers?"

To no one's surprise she answered, "Superheroes."

"Marvel it is."

I selected a movie at random, then we settled in to watch it. After a few minutes I saw Bella relax onto the couch, her attention on the film. I suppressed a smile, glad I'd been able to get her to loosen up just a little bit.

By the time the movie was finished, I was ready to settle down with a book and read before bed. After a long debate we decided that she was sleeping on the couch, so I set it up with sheets and a blanket, then bid goodnight to Bella after encouraging her to make herself at home. Her phone rang after I went to my bedroom, and I heard her speaking in a low voice, although I couldn't make out the words.

I was used to living alone, so I thought that having Bel-la here would be uncomfortable, but for some reason it wasn't. My last thought as I fell asleep was that I wondered how long she'd be here before McMurphy made a move. I was pretty sure he just wouldn't give up. I only hoped that Bella wouldn't be hurt when it happened. Or me.

The next day when Bella and I arrived at the school we were greeted by a giant man. He was tall, at least six five, and he had the broadest shoulders I'd ever seen. He was incredibly handsome – even as a lesbian I could appreciate that -- with kind eyes and a crooked smile.

"You are Lucy, yes?" he asked in a deeply accented voice, reaching out to shake my hand. His hand was so large my entire hand and wrist disappeared in his grip. "I am Boris."

Bella made that weird hissing noise again, which made both of us look at her.

"Ah yes Bella, I understand you," Boris said, taking a step back.

I looked between them in confusion. "What are you talking about?"

"Do not worry my new friend," Boris said, adding extra emphasis on the word *friend.* "Bella and I will take care of everything and keep you safe."

"You're going to be working next door with my friend Elena," I told Boris as we walked down the hallway to the classrooms. "She's the other kindergarten teacher."

"What is this kindergarten?" Boris asked, sounding out the unfamiliar word carefully.

"It's the very first year of school," I explained. "When kids are five years old, they go to kindergarten and that prepares them for first grade, or primary school."

Boris nodded, but he suddenly seemed distracted. He inhaled sharply, his eyes darting around, spine ramrod straight.

"What is it, Boris?" Bella asked, looking around to see what was distracting the bear shifter.

"The smell... my bear is...," he paused, then zeroed in on the door to the classroom next to mine. "Mine!"

Boris thundered off towards Elena's door with Bella and I right behind him. He slammed the door open and skidded to a halt just inside the classroom. Elena jumped up from her desk, her eyes widening in shock. I'd never seen my friend look so disconcerted in all the years I'd known her.

"Mate!" Boris grumbled, his deep voice vibrating through the silence.

"Oh no!" Elena said firmly, holding her palm out as if to ward off his approach even though he hadn't moved. "No, no. Don't even think about it, bear."

"What's happening right now?" I asked.

"Boris is Elena's fated mate," Bella explained.

"I don't know what that means, not exactly."

"This woman, Elena, she is the one I will spend my life with. Is like soulmate is to human," Boris explained, although his eyes never left Elena's. "She is mine. I am hers. We will make big, strong cubs together."

“Oh no we won’t,” Elena said, giving him a glare that would hobble a lesser man. “I don’t believe in that mate shit. And I’m not going to be your brood mare.”

“What is brood mare?” Boris asked in confusion.

“I have a career and a life,” Elena said firmly. “I am not giving that up to be barefoot and pregnant, cleaning your house and birthing your big headed bear babies.”

“You cannot fight fate,” Boris replied, his tone turning stubborn.

“Watch me.”

I still wasn’t clear about this mate stuff, but one thing was for sure, if Boris thought winning over Elena would be easy, he was dead wrong. I’d known my best friend since we were assigned as roommates freshman year of college, and there was no one more stubborn than Elena.

The bell rang, startling all of us.

“The kids will be here soon,” I reminded Elena. “Will you be okay with him?”

Elena looked from me to Boris and back again.

"I'll be fine," she said. "We need to focus on the kids right now. If you have any trouble next door, give us a holler and we'll be right over."

"We will," I promised.

As I walked away I heard Elena say, "Listen bear, in this classroom I'm the boss. You listen to me and do whatever I say, understand?"

"Of course my mate," Boris said easily. "You are alpha here. But I will be alpha at our home."

The last thing I heard was Elena's gasp of outrage.

Bella

Well this was turning out to be a banner assignment. To my knowledge we'd never had two agents find their mates on the exact same job. Lois was going to have a stroke. Despite the fact that she'd found her own mate while working, it pissed her off to no end that her agents continued to fall for their clients.

As if any of us had a choice. Lois was a wolf shifter, she knew as well as the rest of us that fate didn't care about what you wanted or whether it was a convenient time to find your mate.

I did however need to come clean to Lois about Lucy being my mate. It would be way worse for me if my boss found out later. And she would find out. Nothing got past Lois. Maybe I'd tell her tonight.

We got through our morning class without incident, then had a very awkward lunch with Elena and Boris in the teacher's lounge. Poor Boris was following Elena around like a puppy while she completely ignored him.

Finally Lucy said, "Elena I need to show you something in my classroom. Why don't you join me?"

Boris and I both stood up and Lucy wagged her finger at me. "You two stay back."

"That's not going to happen," I said at the same time that Boris growled, "No."

"Fine, then you two stay in the hallway while we talk."

The four of us headed back to the two kindergarten rooms, then Boris and I paced outside while the two women spoke about whatever it was they had to discuss. I had a feeling it was one or both of us.

"So Elena is your mate, huh big guy?" I finally asked.

Boris stopped pacing, then rubbed the back of his neck with his hand. "I thought when I find mate, is easy. This is why we come to this country, to find mate. If mate is human, you expect some problems, but Elena is shifter too, she understands rules."

I noticed that his accent seemed to get thicker when he was upset.

"Don't worry, she'll come around. You can only fight fate and biology for so long."

"And what of you and Lucy?" he asked.

I didn't bother denying that she was my mate. "She doesn't know yet."

"You must tell her," Boris said.

"I never expected to find a mate, but if I did, I sure didn't think she'd be a human."

Boris gave me a smile. "It will work out for you, like your friends. But now we must keep them safe, focus until threat is past."

I didn't bother to remind him that our job was to keep Lucy safe, not Elena. She was under our protection now too, whether she needed it or not. Her being Boris's mate made all the difference.

Our day ended with another dispute between Boris and Elena. As we exited the building Boris told Elena he would follow her home.

"You're supposed to be guarding the human, not me," she snapped. "I can take care of my damn self."

She glanced over at my mate. "No offense Lucy. You do fine for a human."

"None taken," Lucy replied. "But at night it's only you guarding me, Bella, isn't that right?"

"Affirmative. Boris is off the clock."

"Now I am on Elena's clock," he said.

The two bears were still arguing when Lucy and I got into my car. They didn't even notice that we left.

"Those two are going to kill each other," Lucy remarked as we drove past them. Elena was waving her arms at him while Boris puffed himself up and stared at her with a stubborn look.

"They'll be fucking within forty-eight hours," I said confidently.

"How do you know?" Lucy asked curiously.

"You can't stay away from your fated mate no matter how much you want to. There is such a strong biological pull to claim them, you can hardly think of anything else until it happens."

"Do you have a mate?"

"I have not yet claimed a mate," I answered carefully.

"Do you think you will someday?" she asked.

"I have no doubt of that."

We drove in silence for a while before I asked, "Do you know why Elena objects to Boris? I assume that's what you were talking about earlier?"

I knew it wasn't really my business, but I had to admit that I was curious. Most shifters were thrilled to find their fated mates.

"Yeah, she said bears are very into gender norms."

"Huh?"

The corner of Lucy's lips quirked before she answered, "Male bears like to be the boss, and they have expectations for the females to be sweet, submissive little wifeys. Elena doesn't have a submissive bone in her body, and she's not about to change no matter how incredibly hot and sexy Boris is."

I hissed before I caught myself. "You think Boris is hot and sexy?"

I could have sworn that Lucy was a lesbian. Surely fate wouldn't have matched me up with a hetero?

"Well, objectively, sure. But I was quoting Elena there. I'm a lesbian, so Boris isn't exactly my type."

I let out a breath of relief.

"What is your type?" I asked curiously.

"Do you ask all your clients that question?"

"No," I admitted.

"Interesting."

When Lucy didn't say anything else I let the subject drop. For now.

"I'm going to make something for dinner," Lucy announced when we walked into her apartment. "We need more than fries and popcorn like last night."

I held up my hand, gripped her wrist, and waited to respond until I'd scanned every room in the apartment, Lucy trailing behind me.

"You don't have to cook for me," I replied after I'd cleared all the rooms. "I have food."

She put her fists on her hips, the movement making her shirt stretch across her breasts in a way that I didn't hate. I stared at them for a long moment, totally mesmerized.

"What food do you have in that tiny little container in the fridge?" she asked.

"Protein bars, cheese sticks, and blood."

Lucy rolled her eyes. "You're eating chicken. Unless you're a vegetarian?"

"Vampires are never vegetarian," I told her, following her into the kitchen.

I watched as she pulled out a variety of pans and ingredients. She rebuffed my offer to help, so I opened up my laptop and sat at the kitchen table, telling myself that I would at least get some work done. But with my mate moving around the kitchen humming to herself, there was no way I could focus on anything else. I just stared at her like a big sap.

"What's the story with the blood?" she asked, giving me a glance over her shoulder from where she was cooking chicken breasts in a pan. "You said you usually only need a shot of it a day?"

"Yeah, we need a little boost to keep our bodies functioning. There are some substances our bodies don't make by themselves that we get from blood," I explained. "For us, having blood is equivalent to human diabetics who need an insulin shot every day."

"Do you like the taste of it?" she asked.

"I don't hate it," I said. "But we mostly drink donor blood that's been stabilized for storage. It's not as good as fresh blood. I really just think of it like medicine."

"How long can you go without it?" she asked.

"We start feeling sick after a few days or a week, depending on the vamp and how healthy they are. If we go long enough without blood, we will eventually die."

"Hmm."

I couldn't tell what that sound meant.

"A lot of humans get grossed out by the idea of us drinking blood," I offered.

Lucy laughed, her entire face lighting up. My breath caught in my throat. She had such a beautiful smile.

"I'm not like a lot of humans. Besides if you spend enough time in a kindergarten classroom, you get to the point where literally nothing can gross you out. The stories I could tell you..."

Lucy

I covertly studied Bella across the table as we ate our dinner, replaying the conversation I'd had with Elena this afternoon.

"What's going on with you and Boris?" I asked. "The vibes between you are so strong even I can feel them and I'm a human. Aren't you supposed to be happy to find a mate? I've heard your mother nagging you about that more than once."

"Look, maybe it will be different with you and Bella, but for bears, the mating relationship is way too traditional. I've never wanted a mate, and I still don't," Elena said. "Sure, my bear wants to throw him to the ground and ride him, but if Boris and I get together, eventually he's going to resent me.

I can't be the sweet little submissive wife he wants. We'll be fighting all the time, and I don't want to live like that."

"Boris actually said he wants a sweet little submissive wife?" I asked in surprise. He didn't seem to be a misogynist, especially with the way he deferred to Bella.

"No, but I know how bears are," Elena said emphatically.

I started to argue with her then decided against it. I mean, what did I know about bears anyway? Then something she said struck me.

"What did you mean when you said it may be different with me and Bella?"

Elena's eyes widened. "Um, nothing."

"Are you saying that Bella and I are somehow fated mates?" I asked.

"Um. No, I'm not saying that. I'm not not saying that either," Elena stammered, looking uncomfortable. "You really need to talk to her about this."

It wasn't lost on me that when I'd asked Bella if she had a mate she said she hadn't claimed a mate yet. Then again, she hadn't flirted with me. Hadn't given me any 'accidental' touches. She barely made eye contact. She didn't seem at all interested in me – which was a shame, because I'd never been so attracted to anyone in my entire life.

Of course Bella was here for a job. Who was I to expect something more? Was I really upset that she was acting like a professional instead of hitting on me?

Yes, yes I was.

"Tell me more about fated mates," I asked Bella. "Like how do you know when you've found that person?"

She gave me a startled look, then carefully put down her fork. For someone who said she'd be 'fine' with a protein bar, she was putting away quite a bit of my baked chicken and vegetables.

"Well, not everyone has fated mates although we all hope it will happen to us. It's super common in the shifter world for some reason, and less common for the other beings, but not completely unheard of," Bella said. "But it works similarly for all of us. The first hint is the scent. Your other half catches the scent of its mate and starts to get excited, like you saw with Boris today. The first time you touch each other, it's confirmed. There's this feeling of euphoria and rightness that floods you, and almost a kind of relief that you've finally found the person you're meant to spend the rest of your life with. It's... intense."

"You sound like you speak from experience," I prompted.

Instead of answering me, Bella got up and started gathering the dishes. "I'll clean up since you cooked."

I grabbed my e-reader and settled on the couch to read for a while, strangely disappointed by my conversation with Bella. After a few minutes she came out with her laptop, settling on the other side of the couch and tapping away at the keys as she immersed herself in work. Or whatever she was doing.

I heard the loud popping noise half a second before the window shattered. Before I took my next breath I was dragged to the floor and shoved behind the couch. In the distance, I heard the sound of squealing tires.

"Stay down!" Bella ordered, her voice cool and calm. "Don't move."

I stayed behind the couch but shifted enough to watch as she belly crawled over to the window, seemingly oblivious to the broken glass on the floor, then crouched by the window. There was a gun in her hand that I didn't even know she had. She looked out, her head swiveling back and forth before she finally stood up and walked back over to me.

“They’re gone,” she said. “I heard the car drive off, but I wanted to make sure.”

I sat up and Bella squatted down, placing her hands on my shoulders. She’d transformed, I realized. Bright white fangs pressed against her lower lip, now a blood red color instead of its normal lighter red. Her skin had paled until it was almost translucent, and the whites of her eyes had turned red.

“Are you okay? Were you hurt?”

“I’m fine.” I was surprised how shaky my voice sounded. “But they could have killed us.”

Bella shook her head. “It was a message. They want us to know that they’re watching you and they know where you live. The bullet hit the top part of the window, over our heads if we’d been standing. And it was one shot. If they wanted to hurt us, there would have been a spray of bullets to make sure they got us. I need to call this in to my boss.”

She stood up and pulled me to standing. I glanced down and realized that her black tee shirt was wet. Without thinking, I pulled it away from her skin, causing Bella to wince.

"What the... you're bleeding!"

"I must have picked up some glass shards," she said dismissively.

I grabbed her wrists and spread her arms, noting that she had multiple small cuts along her forearms too.

"Come into the bathroom so I can clean these for you," I ordered.

"I need to call Lois."

"You can call her while I work on your wounds." When she just stood there, I employed the 'you're in big trouble now' voice I used in the classroom. "Move. Now."

Bella blinked but followed my instructions.

When we got to the bathroom I made Bella sit on the lid of the toilet, then I grabbed the first aid kit and dropped to my knees in front of her. This close I could see that the pulse in her neck was beating frantically, which I assumed was from the adrenaline of what happened. Her fangs had receded, and her skin, eyes, and lips had returned to their normal coloring.

"Take off your shirt."

"Wh—what?" It was the most unsure I'd ever seen her.

"I need to see what's happening under there. If we don't clean your cuts you could get an infection. You're wearing a bra, right?"

"Yeah."

"Then quit being difficult. Strip."

Bella pulled off her tank, tossing it into the sink, and I examined the cuts on her belly and arms. A couple of them were deep. Not deep enough to need stitches, but deep enough to be bleeding pretty heavily. I grabbed a few packets of antiseptic cleaner and got to work.

"Ow, damn it!" Bella hissed in pain as the antiseptic touched one of the nastier cuts.

"Aren't you a big bad vampire bodyguard?" I asked in a teasing voice. "Quit being such a baby."

I focused my attention on cleaning the wounds, doing my best not to admire the silky smooth skin of Bella's tight abs, or the womanly curve to her waist. I could feel her watching me, but I pretended not to notice.

We both jumped as her phone rang. Bella fished it out of her pocket, then winced when she saw the screen.

"Hi boss," she greeted. "Yeah, I was just about to call you... she's fine... I'm fine, just picked up some glass shards. Lucy is cleaning them right now."

Bella's eyes came to me, then skittered away. "She's not going to agree to that... then they'll just find her at the school... there's no way she'll agree to going into hiding... yeah I can suggest it."

I loved that Bella already knew me well enough to know I wouldn't abandon my kids.

"I'm not running away," I said loud enough for Lois to hear me. "My kids need me."

"Okay, I'll tell her." Bella pulled the phone away. "Lois really thinks we should go to a safe house where we can protect you better."

"No way," I said. "I will not let these people push me out of my own home."

I continued working on Bella's wounds while she talked with her boss. I couldn't understand exactly what was happening on the other end of the call, but Lois sounded annoyed based just on her tone. Or maybe that was her default.

"Yeah, if we could get someone to board it up tonight that would be great," Bella said. "Yeah... okay... I promise. Bye."

"We've got some glass guys that Lois can call to deal with the window," Bella told me as she set her phone down on the counter. "They'll have to board it up in the meantime though."

I applied the last Band-Aid, then settled my hands on her thighs. "I think I got them all," I said. "Maybe next time go around the glass though."

"I didn't even feel it," Bella said. "I was too focused on your safety."

She looked down at me and our eyes met and held. The bathroom suddenly seemed warm, the small space closing in around us as we continued to stare at each other.

"Are you sure you're okay?" Bella whispered.

"Yeah. Are you sure you're okay?" I asked.

"Yeah."

I swayed forward slightly, as if pulled by a string, and Bella leaned towards me. Our faces were only a few inches apart now, and my breathing began to quicken. Bella slowly lifted one hand to cup my cheek, and I relaxed against her palm. I could tell by the flare in her eyes that she liked that.

Then I threw caution to the wind and pressed my lips against hers.

Bella

I growled deep in my throat, searching for control, but there was none to be had. Not when my mate was finally kissing me. I slid my hand from her cheek to the back of her head, bringing her closer, then pressed the tip of my tongue against the seam of her mouth, demanding entrance.

When Lucy opened for me, the kiss turned immediately hot. Our tongues dueled as we explored each other's mouths. My nipples hardened to sharp points, pressing against the fabric of my sports bra, and when Lucy's small hands explored the naked skin of my lower back I almost came on the spot. My heart was pounding so hard I almost felt dizzy.

Bite her. Mark her. Claim her.

My inner vampire's voice was insistent. She didn't want us to let this opportunity pass us by, afraid that Lucy would come to her senses. But when the fabric of Lucy's shirt rubbed against one of the larger cuts on my stomach, making the cut throb, common sense returned to me instead.

If I made love to her now – and I wanted nothing more than to make love to her now – we'd be in bed for days. I knew instinctively I wouldn't be able to let her go until I'd marked her and made her mine so many times that there was no way any creature in this universe would not understand that Lucy was my mate, even Lucy.

As foreign as this possessiveness was to me, I still had the soul of a soldier, a soldier who had a job to do. I couldn't compromise this mission. If I did, my mate could be injured or killed. It was too much of a risk.

Reluctantly I pulled back from the kiss, my lips quirking as I heard the huff of annoyance from my mate.

"What's the matter?" she asked, looking a little dazed.

I loved that I'd been the one to put that look on her face.

"We can't do this," I said gently.

The dazed look was replaced with a combination of hurt and insult.

"You're not attracted to me?" she asked.

I almost laughed at the ridiculousness of the question. Did she think I could kiss her like that if I wasn't?

"That kiss was so hot my skivvies are ruined," I said. "I want you more than I want my next breath. But I'm here to protect you, Lucy. I can't get distracted. It's too dangerous. Besides, the glass crew will be here soon."

I thought she'd argue, but instead Lucy pressed her hands against my thighs, using them for leverage to push herself back up to standing. The strong scent of her arousal surrounded me, and it was all I could do not to pull her back to me.

I just needed to be patient. I'd have my mate when the time was right.

Lucy left the bathroom without another word. The glass crew arrived a few minutes later, measuring for a replacement window and boarding up the space in the meantime. Lucy stayed in the kitchen, tapping away at her laptop, then bid me goodnight as soon as they left, claiming to be tired. A few minutes later I heard the shower running.

I could tell she felt awkward about what happened earlier, but I didn't know how to make it better. Wanting to distract myself from my misery, I texted Boris.

Bella: ***How did it go with your mate?***

Boris: ***I am home with my brothers. Elena refused to let me stay with her. I do not understand. I am a good male.***

Bella: ***Lucy says she's afraid you're one of those chauvinist bears who's going to want her to stop working and have a bunch of cubs.***

Boris: ***I can care for my mate. She does not need to work.***

Bella: ***And that's exactly why she's avoiding you. You need to get with modern times, my friend. Your mate is a strong, independent woman. She wants a career. You need to respect that.***

Boris: ***I will consider your advice. How are things over there?***

Bella: ***Someone sent us a message by shooting out the front window. Lucy of course refuses to go to a safe house or skip work tomorrow.***

Boris: ***We both have strong, independent women for mates.***

Bella: ***How did you know she's my mate?***

Boris: ***It was obvious to me, as it was to Elena. There is one thing where my mate and I are in agreement.***

Bella: ***What?***

Boris: ***I think the American phrase is 'you have your work cut out for you'***

I slept like shit on Lucy's couch that night. I was on edge all night, wondering if McMurphy would do something else, and I woke up grumpy. Well, grumpier than usual. I wasn't a morning person at baseline and getting up in time to be at the school by eight-thirty was killing me.

Smelling coffee, I stumbled into Lucy's kitchen in search of caffeine and a shot of blood. She was standing in front of the coffee pot, watching it intently as if her life depended on it filling faster. The sight of it almost made me smile. Almost.

"Morning," I said.

"Morning," she grumbled back.

My mate hadn't slept any better than I had. With my enhanced hearing I could hear her tossing and turning in her bed for hours last night. Somehow I knew her discomfort was about the kiss, not about her broken window. At least I wasn't the only one suffering.

The suffering is entirely your fault, my vampire reminded me, sending a clear sense of irritation in my direction. For a being who normally only spoke a few words a week to me she was suddenly all sorts of chatty now that we'd found our mate.

"What's our next step?" Lucy asked after we'd both got our coffee and sat down at the table.

I downed my shot of blood before answering. Lucy stared at my lips.

"What?"

"You've got a... uh, you've got a blood mustache."

I felt heat creep up my face, which was strange because as a rule, vampires didn't blush. Or get embarrassed. I grabbed a napkin and wiped off my mouth.

"After school today we're going to head over to the Sapphic Security offices and figure out a plan," I told her. "I don't like sitting around waiting for this guy to make a move."

"Maybe we can smoke him out," she suggested.

"This isn't a movie, Lucy. McMurphy is a hardened criminal commanding a large team of miscreants who obey his every order without question. The only good thing here is that he doesn't want you dead."

"How do you know that?"

"If you're dead, there's no one to tell him where his wife and kid disappeared to," I reminded her. "His focus on you proves he doesn't know who else is involved."

"I technically don't know where they are," she said.

"That won't keep him from doing his best to snatch you so he can try to torture information out of you."

Lucy got a stubborn look on her face that I didn't like. I didn't know what she was thinking, but whatever it was, I needed to put a stop to it.

"No."

"No, what?" she asked.

"Whatever you're thinking, you're not going to do it."

"You have no idea what I'm thinking," she protested.

"I don't need to know what it is to know it's a bad idea," I shot back.

"It's not a bad idea. I was just thinking that maybe we should set a trap for McMurphy. Let him grab me, then you and the team swoop in and take him out."

"No." My tone brooked no argument, but of course, that didn't deter Lucy.

"I think it's a good plan."

"It's not," I said firmly.

"It's my life," she said, her voice rising in irritation. "I'm not going to go on living like this, having a bodyguard, having guys shoot out my windows, looking over my shoulder all the time. This has gone on too long."

Now I was as angry as she was. "Too long? It's been like four days!"

"Four days too long!"

"No mate of mine is going to offer herself as a damned decoy," I yelled. "I forbid it."

"Mate?"

Oh shit.

Lucy

The look on Bella's face was priceless. It was a combination of pissed off and mortification.

When she didn't say anything I prompted, "Did you just call me your mate?"

Bella sighed deeply, took a long swig of her coffee, then set her cup down and gave me an earnest look.

"You're my fated mate, Lucy," she said.

Elena had implied that we were mates, but I thought she was mistaken. Based on Bella's face, maybe she thought it was a mistake too.

"You don't look very happy about that," I noted, feeling a stab of hurt.

"It's not that I'm not happy about it," she said. "I just, well I never really thought I'd find a mate. I was never one of those supes who goes around pining and hoping to find someone. Plus the timing is bad."

"So what are you saying? I'm inconvenient?"

I took a sip of coffee to try to dislodge the lump in my throat. I'd had a history of dating women who didn't want anything long term with me. I was the woman people dated right before they found the love of their lives. The idea that Bella and I were fated to be together -- that there was someone who would love me and not reject me – it had filled me with the most intense sense of euphoria.

Until she opened her mouth and ruined it, that is.

I'd been around Elena's bear family long enough to understand the basics of fated mates, even if I'd assumed it was all a shifter fairy tale. But seeing how it was for Elena and Boris helped explain what was happening with me and Bella. It explained the intense attraction that I felt for her, and presumably she felt for me. It explained why every time we touched, even by accident, it was like a bolt of lightning racing through my body. But it didn't explain why she was rejecting me.

"I'm not rejecting you, Lucy. I'm just saying that we should table this whole mate thing until after you're out of danger. Then we can figure out if this is real and if it can work. I might just be imagining it or something."

She thought it was a mistake?

"Fine," I said, standing up so abruptly I overturned my chair. "I need to get ready for work."

"Lucy..." Bella tried to catch my wrist as I walked by, but I pulled away.

"Get dressed Bella. We need to get to school."

We were both quiet on the way to the school. Every few minutes I'd see her glancing over at me, but I pretended not to notice. I felt raw emotionally. Not just because the person I was quickly developing feelings for, the person who was supposed to love me unconditionally according to their supernatural lore, was rejecting me. It was also because Bella stubbornly refused to even hear my ideas about trapping McMurphy and putting an end to things.

I started to wonder if this had been worth it. I could have just reported the child abuse to social services and moved on. But then I remembered what Suan McMurphy said before she left with the domestic violence counselor.

"You're saving my life, Lucy. He was going to kill me eventually. I told myself it was okay, as long as my son had a good life. But now that I know what he's capable of, that he'll hurt our child too, I know you're saving both of us. I'll never be able to thank you enough. I swear I won't waste this new chance you've given us."

Picturing the look of relief and appreciation on that poor woman's face as she thanked me, knowing that her little boy would grow up in a home free of violence, that's what would sustain me, no matter what happened next.

When we got to school I went right to Elena's classroom to check on her. Boris was there already, standing against the back wall, arms folded over his chest like a giant grumpy sentry as he watched Elena work. Meanwhile, she was studiously ignoring him.

"Hey."

Elena jumped up and gave me a hug.

"How are you? I heard they shot out your window?"

I glanced over my shoulder at Bella, who shrugged.

"It's fine Elena. We weren't hurt. Bella said they were just sending me a message."

"That's not a message I like," she growled. "I could rip that man's throat out."

I could tell by the flicker of her animal behind her eyes that she wasn't kidding. The first time I saw her eyes do that I almost peed my pants. Elena took me outside and made me watch her shift so I could see that she was in total control and would never hurt me, even when she was in her bear form.

"You should come stay at my house," Elena said. "It's safer there."

Elena lived in a good sized house about thirty minutes from here. It was on a double lot that was completely fenced in and surrounded by forest on two sides.

"Yes, this is good idea," Boris called from the back of the room. "We all will stay at Elena's den."

Elena sent him a look that would hobble a lesser man.

"One bodyguard at my house is more than enough, thank you."

The way she sneered 'thank you' made it sound much more vulgar, like maybe she wanted to replace the first word with another word. Perhaps one that started with an F.

"Actually, I think that's a great idea," Bella said. "Boris and I can keep both of you safe that way."

"I don't need a vampire to keep me safe," Elena snapped. "Or a giant idiot."

The giant idiot in question moved to stand next to Bella in solidarity. I rolled my eyes so hard I swear I strained a muscle.

"It's a miracle you and I have managed to live on our own all these years, Elena," I said sarcastically. "Good thing we have our mates to tell us what to do now."

Elena's eyebrows rose. "Oh, so the vampire finally told you that you're her mate?"

"Yeah, but apparently it's not a convenient time for us to be mates."

Elena huffed angrily, clearly not seeing the parallels between my situation and how she'd treated Boris. The giant man stepped closer and put one meaty paw on my shoulder.

"Is very hard to be rejected by mate," Boris told me sympathetically. "I know this pain very well."

Elena growled at him, but I wasn't sure if it was because of his words or because he was touching me. I didn't have time to find out. The bell was ringing, and I needed to get to my classroom to greet the kids as they arrived. All this drama could wait for later.

The first part of the morning passed quickly. No one cried or threw up or had a tantrum, which was a good day in the world of kindergarten. The weather was unseasonably warm, so Elena and I took our two classes outside for recess instead of going to the gym like we did most days.

As per our protocol, Elena stood at one corner of the playground, with me at the other. We positioned Boris and Bella at the other corners so we could carefully watch everything that was going on with the kids. When both classes were outside together, we had over forty kids to keep track of. The more eyes on them, the better.

I was leaning against a fence near a tree when I heard a voice behind me.

"Do not turn around. Don't make a sound or I'll shoot you, hear me?"

I stiffened, easing away from the fence slightly and nodding my head. My eyes darted to Bella and then to Boris, but they both were distracted by the kids.

"My boss has lost patience. If his family isn't returned to him within twenty-four hours, you will be dealing with him. Then you will pay. Slowly and painfully, over and over again until they are returned. Do you understand?"

I knew I should play along. Be passive. Not irritate the man who presumably had a gun. But I didn't have it in me.

"Tell your boss if he wanted a family, he shouldn't have hit them. There's a special place in hell for child abusers and wife beaters. I only hope he visits there soon to see for himself."

"It's your funeral, lady." Maybe I was imagining it, but I could swear I heard grudging respect in the goon's voice.

I looked around the playground again, and my eyes locked with Elena's. Whatever she saw, it made her come racing over, Boris and Bella in close pursuit. I turned as I heard the sound of a car door slamming and tires squealing. I tried to get a look at the license plates or any information on the car, but they moved by too fast.

"I go," I heard Boris yell to Bella. "You guard mates."

My mouth dropped open in shock as Boris took a flying leap, vaulting over the six foot chain link fence and chasing after the car at top speed. I had no idea the man could move that fast.

"What happened?" Bella demanded as she and Elena reached me at the same time.

"The kids."

They turned at my reminder and we saw forty sets of eyes staring at us curiously.

"Everything is okay," I called. "Miss Bella and Miss Elena were having a race. Miss Elena is the winner. Now let's finish our play time before we have to go back inside."

The kids returned to running around the playground and I watched them carefully while updating Bella and Elena on the exchange with McMurphy's goon. When I shared what I'd told the man, Elena burst out laughing.

"It's not funny," Bella growled. "She doesn't need to be antagonizing the fucking mafia!"

"Language," I reminded her.

My vampire bodyguard just glared at me.

"Well, there's two things I know for sure now," Elena said. "First, you have lady balls of steel my friend. And second, for a bear, that Boris is freakishly fast."

Bella

We were just about to take the kids back inside when Boris returned. He was moving slowly now, a look of irritation on his face. We met him at the gate, Lucy unlocking it for him, and when he entered the schoolyard I saw that he was limping a little. His clothes were torn and dirty.

"Are you okay, Boris?" I asked, moving in front of him and touching his arm.

Elena gave me a shove that made me fly a couple of feet in the air, landing on the ground.

"Stay away from him, vampire."

For someone who'd rejected her mate she was a little possessive of him.

She moved closer to Boris, deliberately blocking him from my view. "What happened? Are you injured?"

I waited for Lucy to check on me, but when she barely spared me a glance, I pushed to my feet with a disgusted sigh.

"I catch car," Boris said. "Jump on top but they make car go like this..."

He mimed the driver turning the steering wheel back and forth sharply, making the car careen from side to side.

"I hold on, but then they slammed on brakes, and I go flying over, how do you call it? The hood. They reversed and all I see is dust by the time I get up again."

"Stupid bear," Elena chided. "You could have been seriously hurt."

Boris gave her an arrogant smirk. "It takes more than that to hurt me, mate. Do not worry about me. I am well."

Elena huffed and turned back toward the school, clapping her hands together and raising her voice to be heard. "Okay kids, let's get back to class now."

As we shepherded the kids back into the building I stuck close to Lucy. I couldn't believe that she'd antagonized

McMurphy's man like that. I was half tempted to throw her over my shoulder, take her to one of our safe houses, and lock her inside until we figured out how to catch this guy. But I had a bad feeling that wouldn't go well for me. My mate was tough for a human.

After the school day was over, Lucy and I headed to the Sapphic Security offices. Elena followed us in her car. Apparently she was part of the protective detail now, or at least she thought she was. I didn't even need to look to know that Boris would be close behind her.

When we got to the office we all gathered in the main conference room. Lois was wearing her usual camo pants, black tank top, and shit-kicking boots, a grumpy look on her face even as she tried to smile for our client. Wanda and Martha came in right after, both of them looking around curiously as they picked up on the tense mood in the room.

"Pavlovski! What's going on?" Lois barked.

Despite the fact that I was a vampire and she was a wolf, my vamp cowered inside me. Lois was that much of an alpha.

I briefed the team on the shot out window last night, then shared the threat against Lucy on the playground and Boris's subsequent chase.

"Nice try, bear," Lois said grudgingly.

It was high praise from her, and more than she gave her own employees.

"Is good to show my mate I am strong and can protect," Boris said.

"What?" We all jumped as Lois shouted. "Lucy is your mate? Why does this keep happening with you idiots?"

Elena made a soft growling noise, although I was fairly sure she didn't realize that she was doing it.

"No Boss Wolf," Boris said, using his nickname for Lois. "Elena is one who is my mate. The tiny human belongs to Bella."

"No I'm not!" Elena said at the exact same time that Lucy cried, "I do not!"

My boss's irate gaze moved between the four of us.

"Am I running a security company here or a goddamned dating service?" she asked.

We all knew better than to answer.

"I'm paying you idiots to protect people, not mate them."

"In fairness, it's not like any of us can choose when and how we meet our fated mate," Martha piped up.

Lois sent her a look that made her slide down in her chair a little, her eyes dropping to the table in submission. I was pretty sure she peed herself a little.

"Can we focus on the threat to Lucy, please?" I asked as the tense silence lengthened. "I am not claiming my mate right now, and neither is Boris."

I bugged my eyes out at Boris. "Right Boris?"

He sighed deeply. "Right. We wait until after job."

"You'll wait way longer than that," Elena snapped, but after seeing her reaction to Boris potentially being hurt, I knew that she was going to cave eventually. None of us could fight biology anyway.

Except maybe Lucy.

I'd messed up this morning. I hadn't meant to tell her the way I did, and I certainly never meant to make her feel like I didn't want her. I wanted her all right. I wanted her with every fiber of my being. But I needed to keep all my personal feelings locked away in a box while I focused on my job. McMurphy was escalating, and I couldn't afford to be distracted. After all this was over, I had the rest of my life to win over my mate.

"We need to set up a safe house," Lois said.

Lucy shook her head. "I'm not going to a safe house."

"You can bring your bear friend if you're worried about her," Lois said in a coaxing tone that I didn't know she had in her.

Elena growled again and Lucy patted her arm to calm her.

"Elena can take care of herself," Lucy said. "But we have kids depending on us. We need to be at school. Besides, the guy who threatened me today said I had twenty-four hours. Clearly these guys are going to make a move tomorrow. I say we wait and see what they do."

"No."

This time Elena, Boris, and I all spoke as one.

"With you three around they're not going to get to me anyway," Lucy said, using the same tone she used when she explained to one of her kindergarteners that he couldn't fly. "They'll try something. You'll catch them, and then this will be over. I can go back to living my life, and McMurphy's family doesn't need to live in fear anymore. It's a win-win for everyone."

I was trying to come up with a convincing argument when my boss spoke up.

"Fine, we'll play this your way Lucy. I'm in favor of smoking the asshole out myself, truth be told. But I prefer that you don't stay in your apartment until this is over."

When Lucy started to argue Lois held up a hand. "You have to think about your neighbors. Do you really want them to be hurt?"

My mate deflated a little. "No."

"Come stay at my house, Lucy," Elena offered. "You're already comfortable there and you know it's secure. It'll be like one of our sleepovers. I'll turn on my perimeter alarms, and you'll have me and Bella with you just in case."

My eyes widened as I wondered why a bear who taught kindergarten had perimeter alarms. I'd need to find out more about that.

When Lucy hesitated Elena sighed and said, "You can bring the big guy too."

Lucy gave her a sly smile that made me think her reticence was more about fixing up her friend with Boris than any real fear for her own safety.

"Okay, if we can bring Boris and Bella, I'm in."

"Let's assume that we're right and McMurphy is making his move tomorrow," Lois said, moving on. "He'll likely make his move around the school, especially once he realizes that Lucy is not staying at her apartment."

She studied her laptop for a few seconds. "Gunderson, you'll patrol the perimeter tomorrow," she told Martha. "Diaz, you take the comms van and monitor the agents. Maybe do some of that web voodoo and see if you can track McMurphy's movements."

Wanda's 'voodoo' was actually her strong hacking abilities. She spent more time in the office monitoring computers than she spent out in the field. Unless of course her partner Tasha Blue was on tour. Then Wanda was assigned as lead protection agent for the musical superstar.

"No problem boss," Wanda replied. "I've already broken into their security system, so I'll know for sure when they're on the move."

"Great. Let's reconvene tomorrow at seventeen hundred hours." She glared at each agent including Boris in turn before adding, "Don't fuck this up!"

Lucy

As the meeting wrapped up, Lois insisted that Martha and Wanda should go to my apartment to pack a bag, concerned about me and Bella returning there in case McMurphy's guys were waiting to ambush us. Bella's coworkers returned faster than I would have expected with a suitcase stuffed with enough of my clothes to last for a week as well as my laptop, phone charger, and toiletries. Anything else I needed I could get from Elena.

After a brief tussle, we decided that the four of us would ride together in Bella's bulletproof Sapphic Security SUV since it was the safest. Boris sat in the front with Bella, the seat pushed back as far as it would go to accommodate his long legs, while I sat behind Boris with Elena next to me. We were all quiet on the drive, presumably lost in thought.

Normally I loved going to Elena's house. It was adorable. With its exterior made of rocks and all the trees around it, her house looked more like a mountain cabin than a suburban home at the end of a quiet cul de sac surrounded by forest. It was the perfect place for her to exercise her bear when the neighbors weren't around.

Elena had four overprotective older brothers, one of whom was a home security installer, so when she bought the house they'd insisted on installing a state of the art security system including perimeter alarms, cameras, and fencing that was technically higher than was allowed. Not that anyone in the neighborhood would have the guts to confront her about it. Elena didn't need any of that, given the fact that she could turn into a giant grizzly bear at will, but her brothers periodically dropped by unexpectedly and she'd learned it was easier to engage her alarm system than argue with them for hours about why she didn't use it.

Bella pulled the SUV into the garage, then Elena showed us around. I'd spent a lot of time there, so I bypassed the tour and went right to the guest room to stow my stuff.

A few seconds later, Bella walked in, carrying her bag that Martha and Wanda had retrieved from my apartment.

"What are you doing?" I asked.

"There are only two bedrooms here," Bella said, setting her bag on the floor in the corner.

Oh crap, I'd forgotten about that when I agreed that we could all stay at Elena's house. Bella's assumption that she could stay with me grated.

"Sleep on the couch then," I snapped.

"Boris got the couch," she said. "He made a play to share a room with Elena, but she threatened to rip his intestines out with her claw, so he agreed to the couch."

"Well, you can't sleep in here," I said.

Bella shrugged. "You want me to sleep with Elena then? There's not enough room for me on the couch with Boris."

For some reason, the thought of Bella sleeping in Elena's bed filled me with a jealous rage, despite the fact that I knew my best friend was unequivocally heterosexual. And clearly smitten with Boris, whether she wanted to admit it or not.

"Fine."

Bella gave me a look. "Your words say 'fine', but your tone tells me something different."

"Look, we'll make do. You were super clear this morning that you're not interested in me being your mate, so that's going to make sharing a room kind of awkward, but let's just agree to maintain a cordial working relationship until this is all over and we can go our separate ways."

Bella's face turned intense, and she stalked over to me. I had the sensation of being prey, yet I stood my ground, not moving.

"I wasn't super clear...," Bella made air quotes here, "that I wasn't interested in being your mate. What I said was, we needed to table any discussion about mating until after you were out of danger."

"You also said you thought you might be imagining it," I reminded her, still feeling the stab of hurt from this morning.

"I misspoke," she said slowly. "I am definitely *not* imagining it."

I shrugged and took a step back. Bella followed me. My heart rate picked up.

"I get it, Bella. I'm not who you would have picked. I'm not convenient. It's not the right time. It's all good. I'm not a clinger. No means no and all that," I said, my voice breaking before I cleared my throat. "I'm not going to harass you about it. I just thought mates were hard to reject, but I guess that's just some shifter fairy tale I heard from Elena's family, because clearly both you and Elena don't have any problem rejecting your mates."

"I'm not rejecting you!" Bella's voice rose, and a flush of pink appeared on her cheeks as she lost a bit of her composure. "If I give in to what's happening between us now, I'll get distracted. If I get distracted, you might get killed! McMurphy might be human, but he's lethal and he commands a small army ready to do his bidding."

"I said it's fine Bella. Just let it go." I pushed past her. "I'm going to see if Elena needs help making dinner."

Before I reached the door Bella grabbed my wrist, swinging me around to face her.

"You are the most stubborn, difficult woman I've ever met," she said, lowering her head so our lips were only a few inches apart.

"Are you sure?" I asked impishly. "Because I've met your boss."

Bella sighed. "Don't bring up Lois when I'm about to kiss you."

"Won't kissing me make you distracted?" I asked, even as my heart started pounding in anticipation.

"Not as much as not kissing you does," she groaned.

Bella released my wrist and brought her hands up to frame my face, holding me still as her lips descended on mine. The last kiss we shared started slow and soft, but not this one. Bella pressed her lips firmly against mine, taking my lower lip between her teeth and biting down hard enough to make my gasp. As soon as I opened my mouth she thrust her tongue inside, dominating me.

I loved it.

I didn't realize she was walking me backwards until I connected with the door. I wrapped my arms around her trim waist, pulling her closer, as I gave myself over to sensation.

As the kiss went on and on, my panties turned damp and I started wantonly rolling my hips against Bella, looking for the pressure that I needed.

Suddenly I heard a thumping noise behind me, making me jump. I pulled away guiltily.

"If you two are done sucking face in there," Elena's voice boomed through the wood. "We need to figure out a plan for dinner."

"Uh. Yeah. Right there," I called, putting my hands on Bella's shoulders and pushing her away from me. My face flamed with embarrassment.

Bella looked a little disoriented, and I felt a sense of satisfaction that I wasn't the only one thrown off kilter by what had just happened.

I couldn't remember any other kiss that had affected me as much as this one – unless I counted the kiss in my bathroom last night. Then I remembered Bella's subsequent rejection.

"If we're going to share a room, we're going to need ground rules," I hissed. "Starting with no kissing."

Bella's expression cleared and she gave me an amused look.

"You seemed to enjoy it just fine." She made a show of sniffing the air. "Smells like it, anyway."

"Don't be gross," I said sternly. "You're the one that said we shouldn't be kissing so I'm going to hold you to it."

At least I hoped I could...

When I got into the kitchen Elena was doing her best to make Boris get out of the kitchen.

"Get out of my space, bear," she snapped, hip checking him as she headed for the refrigerator.

"I am a chef," he said.

Elena paused. "What? I mean, I know you own a restaurant, but I thought you were an agent with Sapphic Security and the CIA?"

"My brothers and I do contract work for Lois. And others. But our main job is cooking at restaurant."

"Cooking at restaurant?" Elena repeated like she thought maybe he'd used the wrong English word.

"The bears have a great little diner up the street from Angie's wife's bakery," Bella piped up.

"I know," Elena said. "I just assumed it was an investment. I didn't think that they actually did any of the cooking."

"We do cooking. We trade food for cupcakes," Boris said. "Suzie makes honey cupcakes special for us."

Elena perked up. "Honey cupcakes? Yum."

One thing about those bears, they loved their honey.

"I bring you honey cupcakes," Boris said, his accent seeming to thicken as he spoke. "First, I make you Belarusian meal. You will like."

When Elena just stood in the kitchen staring at him, he placed his hands on her shoulders and led her out of the kitchen.

"You entertain guests now."

Quit telling me what to do," she grumbled as she left the kitchen.

I suppressed a smile. My best friend had met her match.

Bella

After a delicious meal of Belarusian dishes I couldn't pronounce, Lucy and I headed out to the back deck to have an after dinner drink with the bears. Elena and Lucy shared a bottle of wine while Boris and I opted for beer. The two bears seemed to have declared a temporary truce, likely brought on by food. Elena hadn't been able to hide how much she enjoyed everything that Boris cooked for us, and for his part, Boris looked proud as a peacock.

"It's so nice out here," Lucy said wistfully. "I wish my place had outdoor space like this."

I bit my lip to keep from telling her that after we were officially mated we could find a nice place of our own. I'd never wanted to buy a house before. In the military I'd lived wherever they put me, and once I got out and moved to Seattle to work at Sapphic Security, I'd moved into the first apartment I could find. It wasn't exactly crappy, but it also wasn't particularly nice.

With my mate sitting close to me, I was having a hard time keeping my hands off her. Finally I decided to give in to temptation, sliding my leg closer to hers. When Lucy didn't move away, I stretched my arm over the back of her chair, playing with her golden brown hair. It was soft and silky, and I slid it through my fingers over and over like I was in some kind of a trance.

Lucy didn't react externally, but I could smell the sweet scent of her arousal. When Elena sent her a curious look, I knew the bear could too.

My hand slid across the back of her neck, and I realized that something was missing.

"Where's your necklace?" I asked Lucy.

"What necklace?" she asked.

"The tracker I gave you."

Lucy frowned. "I took it off to shower last night. It must be at my house."

"I told you not to take it off," I reminded her.

"I don't usually wear jewelry in the shower. It was just a habit to remove it with the rest of my jewelry."

I sighed heavily.

"We'll get you a new one when we're at the office tomorrow," I said. "Let's head upstairs. I know you like to read before you go to sleep."

"Do you want me to grab the air mattress from the garage?" Elena asked.

"No," I answered.

"Yes that'd be great," Lucy said at the same time.

I suppressed a sigh. The room had a giant king sized bed, there was no reason we couldn't share it. But I wasn't going to start an argument in front of our friends either. If Lucy wasn't comfortable being in bed with me, she wasn't comfortable.

There was no reason for me to be a jerk, especially after I basically rejected her less than twenty-four hours ago.

After a brief argument Lucy settled in the bed, leaning against the headrest as she read a book on her e-reader. Meanwhile I did some light stretching, then settled down on the air mattress that Elena had inflated for me and set up on the floor. I lay totally still, staring at the ceiling, unable to fall asleep until after Lucy did.

The room was completely silent, silent enough that after a while I became aware of the faint hissing noise. What the hell? I glanced around but Lucy seemed oblivious to it. Maybe I was imagining it.

Thirty minutes later I knew I wasn't imagining it. The air mattress had a leak, evidenced by the fact that it was now almost completely flat. It was fine though. I'd slept on the floor – and other equally uncomfortable places – hundreds of times when I was out on missions in the military.

Lucy got up to use the restroom, returning fresh faced and smelling of mint toothpaste. As she walked by the air mattress, she paused.

"I thought Elena inflated that for you."

"She did," I answered. "It has a leak I guess."

Lucy squatted down and lifted one flattened corner of the mattress.

"You can't sleep on this."

"It's fine. I've slept in way worse places," I reassured her. "I once slept in a tree in the jungle."

"Were you upside down?" she asked.

I looked at her in confusion. "No, I was sitting on a branch with my back against the tree trunk."

Then she giggled, the sound so sweet it made me want to hug her. "It's just that I thought bats slept upside down."

I rolled my eyes. "Yeah yeah, hit me with the vampire jokes now, fine."

Lucy giggled again, then stood up, holding out her hand. "Come on, you can sleep in the bed with me."

"Honestly, I'm fine down here."

She shook her head. "Bella. There's no way I'm going to be able to sleep if I know you're on the hard floor. This bed is huge and super comfortable, we can both enjoy it. On our own sides."

I took her hand and leapt to my feet. "Okay then. What side do you want?"

I was sure I wouldn't be able to sleep, but as soon as I heard Lucy's breathing even out I was right behind her, falling into a deep and restful sleep. As usual, Lucy woke up earlier than me. I heard the sound of her alarm right before she sat up in bed, stretching and yawning. The sun was shining brightly through the window, unusual for Seattle at this time of the year, and I brought the blanket up over my head with a loud groan.

"It's too early."

"Such a cranky vampire," Lucy teased. "Is it because we didn't have the romcom moment last night?"

I lowered the blanket just enough to free my eyes. "Romcom moment?"

"You know, two characters share a bed and start off on opposite sides but by the time they wake up, they're both in the middle of the bed in a tangle of arms and legs, snuggling."

I frowned in confusion. "You want to snuggle?"

"God no, what I want is to pee, and then have some coffee."

She hopped out of bed with way more energy than a person should have for that time of the morning, the movement pulling down her sleep shorts just enough to reveal the very top of her curvy ass. My fangs immediately descended.

Soon, I promised my vampire. *Soon. When this case is over, we will claim her.*

Hopefully Lucy would be on board with that because if she rejected me, I would never recover.

I took a quick shower then headed down to join Lucy in the kitchen. Elena was there, but not Boris.

"Where's Boris?" I asked.

Elena canted her head towards the living room. "Fast asleep leaning against my front door. I have no idea why."

"Oh yeah, he does that sometimes so he can make sure he wakes up if there's an attack."

Boris came in a few minutes later, wearing only sweatpants. His feet and expansive chest were bare, and when I looked at Elena, she was staring at him like a kid with cake. I had a feeling she wasn't going to be able to resist mating with the Belarusian for too long.

"We will review the plan," Boris ordered when he joined us at the table, his coffee cup looking small in his giant hand.

"You're in charge now?" Elena asked sarcastically, taking offense to his tone.

"Yes."

She opened her mouth, but I interrupted. "We will all act like this is a normal day. If there's an attack, our goal is to protect Lucy."

"No," Lucy said firmly. "Our goal is to protect the children. I will not have one of our students injured on my account."

When no one answered she looked us in the eye one by one. "If it's a choice between saving a kid or me, you *will* save the kids first, you hear me?"

We all nodded, but I wasn't sure that any of us wanted to be in the position to make that choice.

As it turned out, none of us had to. We got through the entire school day with no sign of McMurphy or his men. With agents patrolling outside and the four of us on high alert inside the school, the lack of action was almost a letdown. With nothing to debrief on, Lois canceled our meeting and we all headed back to Elena's house, being careful to ensure that we weren't followed. After we scanned her house for listening devices or explosives, we activated the security system and settled in for a weekend sequestered together. Just the four of us.

I had a feeling it was going to be a long weekend.

Lucy

By Saturday afternoon I was going stir crazy. I usually spent my weekends out and about in the community, having lunch with friends, or going to the gym. I couldn't do any of that while we were holed up at Elena's.

Don't get me wrong, I loved spending time with my best friend, and I was grateful that she was letting us use her place as a safe house, but I hated feeling trapped. The presence of our two bodyguards only made it worse.

"I need to go for a run," Elena announced after dinner on Saturday. "My bear is ready to explode."

"I will go with you," Boris said immediately.

"You need to stay with Lucy," Elena reminded him.

"It's fine, Bella can protect me," I said brightly.

I was Team Elena, don't get me wrong, but it was also very obvious to me that Elena was falling for her mate, so I wanted to help her along. Sometimes my best friend was too stubborn for her own good. Plus, Boris seemed like a great guy.

Boris sent me a grateful smile, but Elena shot me a scowl that would make most people wet themselves. I'd seen that scowl before though and it didn't faze me at all. Elena was all bark, no bite. At least with people she cared about.

"You need your exercise," I said patiently. "I'll feel better if I know you've got back up in case someone tries to do something to you. I know you can protect yourself, Elena, but you are not invincible."

I didn't mention that I was hoping that a nice run would do wonders for her bad mood.

"Fine," she grumbled. "Let's go, bear."

Bella and I watched from the deck as Elena left the backyard and headed for the tree line, Boris following close behind her. I heard a loud roaring sound that I was pretty sure was Boris's bear, followed by a softer growl that even I could tell was conveying annoyance. That had to be Elena.

"I hope they don't kill each other out there," I said.

"I've got five bucks they're going to fuck out there."

"You still think that Elena will break?" I asked.

I had my doubts. It was clear to me that Elena was drawn to Boris despite her protestations to the contrary, but my bestie was a very stubborn woman. I wasn't sure that Boris was going to win this battle of wills.

"Their bears will take over while they're out running," Bella said. "They'll be all over each other before they even know what's happening and once they start fooling around, it will be nearly impossible for them to stop."

Sure enough, when Boris and Elena returned an hour and a half later, something was different between them. Elena was still basically ignoring Boris, but her words no longer had any heat. At one point Boris gave her a look that was so intense I almost felt uncomfortable witnessing it. And to my shock, it made my best friend blush. Elena was not a blusher.

When she went to bed, Boris followed her into the bedroom without a discussion. A few minutes later, we heard the headboard pounding against the wall with enough force that I was surprised they didn't break right through. A few times I heard growling.

"Um, they're kind of loud," I noted unnecessarily after a particularly loud thump.

Laying in bed next to Bella listening to our friends have sex was strangely arousing. Maybe because I was imagining what it would be like if it was me and Bella banging our own headboard. The longer it went on, the more aroused I became.

"I can help you with that problem," Bella said suddenly.

I set my e-reader down to look at her. She was on the other side of the bed tapping away at her laptop.

"Help me with what problem?" I asked in confusion.

"You're getting turned on listening to our friends have sex." Bella sounded almost bored.

"Aren't you feeling it too?" I asked. "It's like the world's loudest porno over there."

Bella shrugged. "I'm a supe and a former soldier, I have a lot of self-control."

For some reason I had a feeling she was bullshitting me. I shifted to face her on the bed.

"So if I were to touch you between your legs right now, you wouldn't be wet, is that what you're saying?"

Bella seemed surprised at my calling her out. "Well..."

Before she knew my intention, I reached over and cupped her mound. She was wearing a pair of loose fitting shorts, and I could feel the heat of her through the fabric. Bella's eyes flew to mine, and we stared at each other for a long, charged moment. Then she set her laptop down on the table next to her and opened her legs a few inches.

I resisted the urge to pump my fist in victory. Keeping my eyes on her face, I slowly traced my fingers up her inner thigh before slipping underneath the hem of her shorts. When I found the damp fabric at the apex of her thighs, I couldn't help but smile.

"Someone's panties are wet...," I said in a singsong voice.

Bella winced. "I hate that word."

"Wet?"

"Panties."

"How about we lose them, then?"

Bella's legs snapped closed, trapping my hand between her thighs, and I used my other hand to pinch the fleshy area of her outer thigh. Bella jumped.

"Open," I said in my best bossy kindergarten teacher voice.

I thought for sure she'd put a stop to things but then we heard Elena release a long, throaty moan and Bella's legs fell open again. Grabbing the hem of her shorts, I pulled them down her legs, taking her panties with them. It sounded crazy, but Bella had the prettiest pussy I'd ever seen. Neatly trimmed. A lovely shade of dark pink. And visibly damp.

Not wanting to give her time to change her mind, I slid my fingers inside her pussy lips, stroking her and spreading her moisture as I explored. Bella rocked against my hand, sliding farther down the bed as I continued to explore her folds.

"I want a taste," I said, my voice surprisingly husky.

Spreading Bella's legs wide, I lay down on my belly and licked my way from the bottom to the top of her slit. Bella made a whining noise that turned me on even more. Slowly I licked from bottom to top and back again, exploring every inch of her. I circled her clit on every pass but never touched it. Not yet.

When she was breathing heavily I finally slid first one, then a second finger inside Bella's channel. I watched her carefully, learning what she liked as I roughly fucked her with my fingers. Bella rolled her hips to meet me on every stroke. I shifted so I was pressing my body over one of her thighs, holding her down just a bit, and then I lowered my head to tap my tongue against her clit.

Bella's inner muscles were fluttering now. I added a third finger, stretching her wide, then bent my fingers to connect with her G spot.

"I'm close," she cried out.

That's when I sucked her clitoris into my mouth, the action breaking the last of her control. Bella cried out my name, bucking wildly against me, but unable to move too far with her leg trapped under my body.

As Bella started to come down, I pushed up on my elbows to watch her. She looked beautiful with her head thrown back against the pillows, her eyes closed, face a mask of ecstasy. Her fangs had descended, I realized, her color turning unnaturally pale. The fingernails gripping the comforter on either side of her seemed longer and sharper.

Maybe it should freak me out that this woman could change into something different, something not quite human, but I found myself fascinated more than anything. Maybe it was because I'd been around Elena and her shifter family for so many years. Maybe it was because I'd always had a variety of friends from different backgrounds.

Or maybe it was because I was falling in love with her.

I'd known the woman for less than a week, and I knew almost nothing about her. But that didn't change the way I felt.

And that scared the crap out of me.

Bella

Holy crap. Did that really just happen? Did my little mate really just call me out for being aroused and make me come against her hand? And her mouth? What had happened to my ironclad self-control?

When I finally caught my breath and opened my eyes Lucy was propped up on her elbows between my legs, looking very happy with herself. She deserved to be.

Across the hall the headboard started pounding against the wall again, the sounds of whispered endearments and breathy moans reaching my ears thanks to my enhanced hearing. Boris was a machine. Those two had been going at it for nearly two hours.

"I. Uh. Give me a second and I'll take care of you." Apparently I was at a loss for words.

Lucy pushed up onto her knees, then got off the bed.

"I'm good. I'm just going to wash my hands and get ready for bed."

I watched her leave the bedroom with my mouth open so wide I was surprised I didn't swallow a bug or something. She was 'good'? Who turned down an orgasm?

By the time Lucy came back to bed I was feeling kind of insulted.

"Why don't you want me to get you off?" I demanded as soon as she returned.

She shrugged. "I just don't."

"But why?" I pressed. "I'm good at it, you know. I've had rave reviews from other women I've slept with."

Her eyes flared briefly with something that looked like jealousy.

"I'm sure you are good at it," she said in that same voice she'd used yesterday when one of the kids told her that she had an imaginary friend named Eloise. "But sex doesn't have to be quid pro quo, you know."

"Huh?"

"You don't have to get me off right now just because I gave you an incredible orgasm."

"How do you know it was an incredible orgasm?"

Lucy rolled her eyes. "I was there, remember? You came so hard you almost threw me off the bed. Plus you went all fangy and pale. You totally let go, and it was a beautiful thing to watch. But that doesn't mean you have to feel obligated to give me an orgasm."

"I don't feel obligated," I practically shouted. "I want to get you off."

"Yet you never thought about it until I got you off first, so it can't possibly be that important to you."

Lucy came to the bed, turning off the light on her side, then sliding under the blanket and turning her back to me. I just stared at her back slack jawed for a full minute.

"I thought about it plenty," I finally hissed. "I've thought of almost nothing else since the moment I laid eyes on you. But I have a job to do here. I need to keep you safe."

"Which is why you should go to sleep now," I said. "We're both going to need to be fresh tomorrow. Good night."

I lay there glaring at her back for so long I actually grew tired and fell asleep with the light on.

When I woke up Lucy was gone and the sheets next to me were cold. Knowing that she wouldn't go anywhere, I took a quick shower before going to look for her. She was in the kitchen with Boris and Elena, eating breakfast. Someone, presumably Boris, had made an enormous stack of pancakes, a giant bowl of scrambled eggs, a platter of bacon and sausage. Smaller bowls of mixed fruit were set in front of each place setting.

Nodding in greeting, I went to the fridge to get myself a cup of blood.

"Hungry?" Boris asked as I approached the table.

I slid into the chair next to Lucy, noticing that Boris and Elena were sitting so close that their bodies were plastered against each other.

"Yeah, thanks for cooking."

I grabbed a plate, piling it up with eggs and bacon. I wanted to start with protein before I let myself have the pancakes. Draining most of my cup of blood, I re-filled it with coffee from the carafe on the table. When I looked up, everyone at the table was watching me.

“What?” I asked.

“Most people use cream,” Elena snickered.

“Yeah, well most people don’t catch and eat squirrels but there you go,” I snapped.

“I prefer salmon,” Boris piped up. “Squirrels taste too gamey for me.”

“For fuck’s sake,” I mumbled under my breath.

“Bella is cranky in the morning,” Lucy told them. “It’s best not to talk to her until she’s had a cup of blood, coffee, and some protein.”

My inner vampire preened, happy that our mate had paid attention to what I needed. My human side was just annoyed. I was irate about last night. I mean, sure, I’d had a great orgasm, but Lucy’s rejection afterward really stung.

“What should we do today?” Lucy asked the table.

Boris and Elena exchanged a hot look, leaving no doubt what activities they were hoping to engage in today.

"I thought you didn't want a mate," I said to Elena.

She shrugged. "I don't, but I never said I didn't want to get laid."

Oh that was interesting. I'd thought for sure that Boris marked her last night during one of the like seventeen times they'd had sex.

Boris's expression turned stony. "I *will* mark you and we will be mates."

Elena patted his arm. "Yeah sure, okay."

The rest of the day was painfully slow. Boris and Elena would disappear for a few hours, have loud and enthusiastic sex, then come back looking flushed and sated. Meanwhile Lucy and I knocked around the house, alternating between watching movies and reading, both of us mostly keeping to ourselves. A couple of times I tried to bring up what happened last night, but Lucy refused to talk about it.

It was easily the most boring day I'd had in years. I should have enjoyed the boring while I could, because the next day everything changed...

Monday morning the four of us drove to school in my Sapphic Security SUV, and while I wasn't totally at ease, I wasn't expecting anything to happen at seven thirty in the morning. I was wrong.

The minute we exited the car, we were ambushed. Men popped out from between cars, quickly surrounding us on all sides. Boris, Elena, and I quickly closed ranks around Lucy.

"Give us the girl," one guy said, waving a sawed off shotgun in our direction. "My boss needs to talk to her."

Next to me Boris partially shifted, claws and fur popping out of his hands, but the rest of him remaining human. It was an impressive skill. Most shifters couldn't control their shift enough to remain between forms.

"Told you they were shifters," a voice said.

Looking behind us, I saw that more men had joined us, standing on top of cars. There had to be at least twenty goons here. Sure, the bears and I could probably take them, but with those numbers the chances that Lucy wouldn't get hurt were pretty slim. Where was my back-up?

"Tranqs!"

I turned to shove Lucy to the ground as darts suddenly came flying at us from all directions. I felt a dart pierce my shoulder, then another one hit my flank. Time seemed to slow down as the poison hit my system.

"Mate," Boris mumbled as Elena hit the ground.

Boris was right behind her, falling in a giant heap with several darts stuck in his body.

A dart hit my calf, then another got me right in the ass, piercing the denim of my jeans, and then everything went black.

Lucy

I squatted on the ground, trying to make myself as small as possible as we were barraged with darts. I saw Elena hit the ground, then Boris, and finally Bella went down, hitting the concrete with a sickening crunch.

For the first time since this whole thing started, I was well and truly scared.

A man with a gun stalked over to pull me to my feet. Like all of them, he was dressed all in black, including a black stocking hat, making one guy almost indistinguishable from the other.

"You're coming with me," he said, giving my arm a hard pull.

I resisted crying out. I knew that these were the kind of guys who got off on weakness and fear. I wasn't going to give them the satisfaction though. Besides, now that my bodyguard contingent was gone, I needed to keep my wits about me if I was going to get out of this.

"Wait, let me get my jacket," I said. "It's cold this morning."

The guy stopped long enough for me to scoop up the black leather jacket on the pavement. It was Bella's. She must have dropped it on the pavement when the ambush started. If I was going to die today – and I had a bad feeling that once McMurphy learned that I honestly did not know where his family was he would kill me – at least I'd have something belonging to the woman I loved with me.

That's right. Even though I'd only known her for a week, I was head over heels in love with Bella. I was glad I'd had the opportunity to give her pleasure once before I died. I'd derived as much pleasure from watching her come apart under my fingers and tongue than I would having an orgasm of my own.

I just hoped that she would be okay. And Boris and Elena too. I wasn't sure what was in those tranquilizer darts, but they'd made the three supes drop fast. I was grateful that none had hit me. I was pretty sure that anything that took down Boris would kill me for sure.

Then again, maybe that would have been a better way for me to die. Whatever McMurphy had planned for me wasn't going to be good, that's for sure. The worst part was that I'd left that tracking necklace behind at my apartment so now Sapphic Security would have no way to find me.

Two men shoved me in the back of a black sprinter van, and I cried out as my knees hit the metal bottom. The doors slammed and I hurried over, unsurprised to find that I was locked in. Then I went flying as the van took off.

"Damn it," I cried, settling in the corner and holding onto some kind of hook thing in the floor to keep from being tossed around on the ride.

We drove for at least thirty minutes, and when the van stopped I could tell that we were no longer in the city. The air smelled different, even to me as a human. When the doors to the van opened, my suspicions were confirmed. We were parked in front of a giant house, a mansion really, that seemed to be completely surrounded by forest.

"Come on," one of the guys said, taking my arm. "The boss is waiting for you."

Swallowing down my panic, I swiveled my eyes around, trying to get the lay of the land in case I had the chance to escape. Other than the house, all I could see was trees.

I was led through an obnoxiously ornate foyer and into a library. Shelves lined two sides of the room, filled with books, and a huge wooden desk was in the middle of the room, a wall of windows behind it looking out towards what appeared to be a creek. And more trees.

“Miss Ingram, welcome to my home. You’ve been a hard woman to reach.”

Liam McMurphy gave me a smile that didn’t reach his eyes. He was movie star handsome, with thick dark hair, a square jaw with a little dimple, large brown eyes with ridiculously long eyelashes, and blindingly white teeth. He was tall and fit, with wide shoulders, a narrow waist, and a designer suit that probably cost more than I made in a year as a teacher.

“I don’t know where they are,” I said without preamble.

McMurphy’s eyes narrowed. “I guess we are dispensing with small talk then.”

He pointed at a leather chair situated in front of his desk. “Please, sit.”

Before I could react, I was shoved down into the seat.

"Hey!" I glared at the guy who'd been manhandling me. "Don't be rude."

The guy looked like he wanted to punch me for my insolence, but McMurphy merely chuckled.

"Leave us, Gino."

"I'll be outside, boss."

McMurphy sat behind his desk, clasping his hands together in a pose that I was sure was supposed to be non-threatening.

"Miss Ingram, I acknowledge that I lost my temper with my wife. But I realize the error of my ways now. I'm a changed man, ready to make a fresh start with the woman I love."

"And what about Robbie?" I asked. "Are you ready to make a fresh start with him, as well? I'm sure his bruises have healed by now. Probably not the emotional wounds though."

"Children are resilient, you know this much better than I do," he said smoothly. "I'm willing to do whatever I need to do to make it up to them. Surely you don't want to break up my family? One mistake shouldn't ruin everything."

"One mistake?" I said, pinning him with the look I gave the kids when I knew they were lying. "Is that the answer you're going with?"

I jumped as McMurphy's fist hit the wooden surface of the desktop. "Do not interfere in my family," he hissed. "It will not work out well for you."

"I'm willing to risk that if it means things will work out well for Robbie and his mother," I replied with bravado I didn't really feel.

"Are you telling me that you would die to protect my son and that whore?" he demanded, his voice rising in anger.

I guess we weren't even pretending that he loved his wife anymore.

"I'm a teacher," I reminded him. "We are trained to die protecting our students."

McMurphy gave me a look filled with such malevolence it made me shiver.

"Perhaps I will give you some time to think about your life choices," he said, his voice back to smooth and calm.

"Gino!" he called.

His lackey came into the room immediately.

"Show Miss Ingram to the basement guest room."

I was dragged down a long hallway and then down a staircase to the basement. Gino placed his palm against a reader next to the door in the far corner of the basement, and the heavy door swung open. The room reminded me of a panic room. It was small and square with concrete walls and floors and absolutely no natural light. There was a cot with a thin blanket, a few bottles of water, and a wooden chair in the room. A door on one side led to a half bath with a toilet and sink.

It wasn't exactly the nicest room in the house.

"Enjoy your stay," Gina smirked before he strode out, leaving me alone.

I tried the door, even though I was quite sure it wouldn't open. Then I checked out the tiny bathroom. No place to escape there, not even a window. Nothing I could use for a weapon unless I hit someone with the chair. I picked it up and put it right down. It was heavy, a thick wood like the kind of chair someone's grandmother had in their dining room back in the old country. There was no way I could lift that over my head to hurt anyone.

With a sigh I sunk down onto the chair and took off Bella's jacket. I heard a soft clunk as it hit the floor, then picked it back up to check the pockets.

Holy shit. It was a good thing McMurphy's guys hadn't searched me because this jacket was the motherload. I found a scary looking knife with a retractable blade, a small cannister of bear spray, something that looked like an Air Tag, a protein bar, a small coil of thin wire, and a collapsible cup.

As I got up to get some water from the bathroom sink I wondered if the Air Tag was transmitting. If so, there was a good chance Bella and her team could find me after all. Assuming that they all woke up from whatever they'd been injected with.

Bella

I woke up with a groan. My body felt like it was filled with concrete and my head felt fuzzy. Why was I laying on the cold asphalt of a parking lot?

I shot to my feet as it all came rushing back. The ambush. Boris and Elena going down. The feeling of multiple darts hitting me in quick succession. I started pulling out darts as I looked around, taking stock of my surroundings.

Cars had filled the parking lot, but the area where we were parked was still vacant. Boris and Elena were passed out on the ground. And Lucy... she was gone. Grabbing my phone from my pocket, I crouched down to check Boris and Elena for a pulse.

"Wha--."

I didn't even wait for Lois to finish her greeting before I was giving a report.

"We were ambushed. Lucy is gone."

I forced myself to stay neutral and just give my boss the facts, despite my strong desire to give in to the panic that I was feeling. As a bodyguard I was supposed to stay neutral but there was no way I could stay neutral when some asshole had snatched the woman I love.

"How did they get through you and Boris?" Lois asked.

"Tranquilizer darts, shifter strength," I answered. "I don't know where our back-up is."

"They got stuck behind a wreck," Lois said. "They're pulling in now. All of you get back to the office and let's make a plan to find the client."

"The client is my mate," I snapped.

"And we can't do a freaking thing until you revive Boris and get your asses back here," Lois snapped. "Don't go off half-cocked Bella. These guys are organized. We need a plan."

The sound of tires squealing in the parking lot revived Boris.

"Mate," he mumbled, still feeling the effects of the drugs.

He shimmied over to Elena, then unleashed a torrent of words in Belarusian. I didn't need to know the language to know it was mostly swear words.

"Report!"

Boris and I both looked up as Angie ran over, followed by Martha. I repeated what I'd told Lois while Boris gently shook Elena, trying to get her to wake up.

"What the..." Elena came to, looking around in confusion. "What happened? Where's Lucy?"

"McMurphy got her," I said grimly. "They shot us with shifter strength tranqs. Do you require medical attention, or can you come with us to the Sapphic Security offices?"

Boris pushed up to standing, then grabbed Elena's hand and pulled her up next to him. They both swayed a little but remained upright.

"We go," Boris said firmly. "We need to find Lucy now."

We drove with Martha and Angie to the office and by the time we got there, most of our team was assembled in the conference room. Impatiently I repeated my account of what had happened.

"Where's her tracker?" Lois asked. "It looks like it's at her house and I know they wouldn't have taken her there.

"She took it off before she took a shower and forgot to put it back on," I replied.

Lois huffed out an irritated breath and mumbled something about dealing with incompetence before turning to Wanda. "Do you have any leads on houses?"

My coworker nodded. "Yeah, there about half a dozen houses in a one hundred mile radius that I can tie to McMurphy or one of his shell companies."

She passed around a list.

"It's been nearly an hour," I reminded everyone. "They could be anywhere by now."

"Well the good news is that they need Lucy alive," Wanda reminded me. "He thinks she knows where his family is and as long as she's his only link, he'll keep her alive."

The thought of McMurphy or his men marring even an inch of Lucy's perfect skin made my fangs lower. I'd seen what criminals did with people who didn't cooperate, and it wasn't pretty.

"I'm going through the traffic cams around the school now," Wanda told us, tapping away on her keyboard. "I'll see if I can at least get a hint what direction they were heading."

We all fell silent as she did her magic.

"Well crap," she finally said. "They hit this intersection and then split up in three different directions."

She pressed a button, and the camera feed was projected on the screen on the wall. Five almost identical black SUVs pulled up to the light, then split off, two going in one direction, two in the other, and the fifth car heading off alone.

"Let me overlay the properties we found."

Multiple dots appeared on the screen.

"It looks like these vehicles here on the left, and the ones in the center, are heading towards McMurphy's properties. The cars on the right appear to be going somewhere else."

"Do you know that for sure?" I asked.

She shrugged. "No, it's my best guess."

I resisted the urge to snap at her that I wasn't comfortable with my mate's life depending on Wanda's best guess. My coworker was doing all that she could, I knew that, and she was damned good at what she did. Her instincts were good too.

"I just wish we had a better idea where to focus our time."

We were interrupted by Boris's brothers Yuri and Alexei barreling into the room. Like Boris, they were both tall, wide, and one hundred percent lethal muscle.

"We came as soon as we heard," Yuri said, going to his brother.

Boris stood up, accepting a hug from each of his brothers. The bears might be seasoned operatives with a high body count between them, but they were incredibly sweet and affectionate with the people they loved. Especially each other.

"Yuri, Alexei, I present to you my mate. Elena."

To my surprise, Elena didn't argue. She stood up to offer her hand to the brothers, but instead of shaking it, they pulled her into a hug.

"We have sister now," Alexei said in a voice filled with awe. "We are very happy."

Elena seemed a little flummoxed before saying, "It's nice to meet you both."

"If you damned bears are done with your happy reunion, we have a client to recover," Lois barked.

Every being in the room stiffened at her alpha tone, and Boris's brothers immediately grabbed chairs and sat down at the table, suitably chastened.

"That's better," Lois grumbled. "Now how do we narrow down Lucy's location."

I slipped my phone out of my pocket, thinking maybe there was a ransom request or something, but to my surprise there was a notification of a lost item.

"Your Air Tag is no longer with you."

I opened my phone and toggled over to the 'Find My Phone' app to see where my Air Tag was. I jolted as I realized it was the one I usually kept in my jacket pocket. It was showing a location about an hour away from here.

"Wanda, map this address," I ordered, reading off the location on my app.

"It's one of McMurphy's houses," Wanda confirmed. "It looks like it backs up against the National Forest."

"That's where Lucy is," I said.

Everyone at the table looked at me. "How do you know?" Lois asked.

I held up my phone. "My Air Tag is pinging there. I think Lucy must have taken my leather jacket with her. Either that, or one of McMurphy's guys stole it."

Then I frowned. "It looks like it stopped transmitting about fifteen minutes ago."

"It could be anything," Wanda said quickly. "They could have found it on her and disabled it. The battery could have died. Or they could have her stashed someplace where signals don't get through."

I tried not to think about what kind of place that might be. I'd deal with my emotions later, right now I needed to find my mate.

"We need to roll," I told Lois.

"First, let's make a plan," my boss said firmly. "Then we'll go get your mate."

Lucy

I'd been in the tiny room for about ninety minutes when they came to get me. Either McMurphy was getting impatient, or they figured that trapping me in a windowless room the size of a closet for a while was enough to make me freak out and tell them everything. Sadly for them, all it had done was make me angry.

Two men led me back upstairs. I didn't bother to resist, not when I was outnumbered and didn't have a plan. There was a good chance the agents of Sapphic Security would come for me, but I was also determined to escape on my own if the chance presented itself. I had no idea if Bella was still alive. I had no idea what they'd shot her with. And I doubted that anyone else would think to look for an Air Tag. I resisted touching the pockets of Bella's jacket to confirm that I still had her knife and bear spray there. No sense in making them suspicious.

To my surprise, the men led me to a dining room. McMurphy sat at one end of a long table, another place setting arranged to his right. The table was covered in a pristine white tablecloth, a vase of flowers in the center. Carafes of coffee and orange juice sat alongside plates of breakfast food. It all looked delicious, but I didn't trust these guys not to drug me.

"Miss Ingram, please join me for brunch."

I was shoved down into a chair by one of the guys.

"Leave us," McMurphy dismissed them.

"I find I'm not one for eating early in the morning," McMurphy said conversationally. "I much prefer to eat mid-morning. Please, help yourself to some food. The frittata is delicious."

When I didn't answer, his expression turned dark. Before I realized what was coming, he backhanded me across the face. I cried out as my head snapped back, then I tasted blood in my mouth.

"Answer me," he gritted.

"I'm not hungry," I snapped. "I find that being kidnapped and threatened really messes with my appetite."

McMurphy ignored me, watching me as he ate a piece of perfectly cooked bacon.

"Tell me where my family is and I'll gladly return you to your weird little animal friends."

Like I believed he'd just let me walk away from this. I was a dead woman, unless I escaped or was rescued. And my best chance of either was to keep this guy talking.

"What did you shoot them with?" I asked.

He shrugged. "Just a little tranquilizer. They'll be fine after a nice nap."

At least they weren't dead. I wondered how long the drugs would keep them unconscious though. I had a feeling I didn't have a lot of time before McMurphy started hurting me.

"How did you know they're shifters?" I asked.

"The man flying over a six foot fence and chasing a car was a good clue," he smirked. "And Sapphic Security is well known in certain arenas. Everyone knows they only hire animals for their ranks."

I resisted the urge to chastise him for his... what was prejudice against shifters and supernaturals called anyway? Speciesism?

"They won't be happy when they discover that you took me," I said.

He shrugged dismissively and chewed a bite of toast. "They won't wake up for hours. By then I'll have what I want – one way or another."

"I don't know how to say this any clearer," I said slowly, as if I was speaking to a particularly difficult child. "I don't know where your family is. When they went into hiding, I was not notified of their whereabouts."

"What I'm hearing is either you are willing to die to protect their secret, or you are no use to me," McMurphy said, still in that urbane conversational tone. "Both of those possibilities have one natural conclusion."

He moved quickly, jumping out of his chair and grabbing a fistful of my hair, right by the scalp, and pulling hard. My head whipped to the side, my scalp stinging enough to make my eyes water. It was painful as hell, but I was damned if I was going to give him the satisfaction of covering in front of him.

"Where. Is. My. Family?"

I glared at him with every ounce of fury I could muster. "I. Don't. Fucking. Know."

I thought I saw a brief glimmer of surprise in his eyes. No doubt he wasn't used to defiance. In his position, I was sure everyone catered to his every whim or cowered in fear, as the case may be. It made the fact that his wife left him and took their son even more galling, I was sure.

I didn't realize that McMurphy had partly lifted me off my chair until my ass hit the cushion again. He sat down and took a sip of orange juice. His ability to switch from calm to rage and back again was disconcerting.

He picked up a knife and fork and cut up a half of his waffle.

"One thing I've realized over the years is that people are very fond of their fingers."

He took a bite of waffle and sent me a look I couldn't interpret.

"What?"

"Fingers, Miss Ingram. It's the funniest thing. Even the bravest people lose their determination when I cut off a finger. Or two."

He continued eating his waffle like we were talking about the weather.

"The question is, how much do you like having fingers?"

"As much as you do, I expect."

I had no idea why I was baiting this asshole, but I couldn't help it. Being kidnapped had really pissed me off. And what made me even angrier was thinking about poor little Robbie and his mother living with this sociopathic monster. Not to mention the fact that he'd drugged my friends and the woman I loved with tranquilizer darts. Jerk.

Suddenly there was a crash, and a giant grizzly bear came crashing through the window with a loud roar, sending shattered glass everywhere. Pandemonium broke out. All around I heard the sounds of fighting. Several shots were fired.

As the bear came closer McMurphy leapt to his feet and pulled me toward him, holding me in front of him like a human shield. He had one arm wrapped around my waist like an iron band, and with his other hand he was pressing the barrel of a gun against my temple. He backed up against one wall, keeping me between him and the bear at all times.

There was another crash, and then Bella burst into the room, a gun in hand. When she saw the mob boss holding me at gunpoint, she went full vamp in an instant, fangs descending, eyes turning red, her entire body vibrating with menace.

McMurphy didn't seem at all bothered. His grip on me never wavered, and his breathing remained even. No doubt he figured that he had the upper hand as long as he was holding onto me.

"Release my mate," Bella growled.

I heard McMurphy chuckle like her words amused him.

"The animal thinks you're her mate, Miss Ingram. That's unexpected. I've always heard the vampires stick to their own kind, snobby bastards."

Elena had told me something similar at one point.

"We should see how she likes watching you get your brains blown out."

Bella's gaze didn't waver. To the side, the bear growled menacingly. I knew it wasn't Elena, so I assumed it was Boris.

We were in a standoff.

McMurphy's arm slid up from my waist to wrap around my upper chest and shoulder. In the distance, I could hear more fighting as what I presumed was the rest of the Sapphic Security team fought McMurphy's men.

Bending my wrist, I slowly slid my hand back until I could reach into the side pocket of the jacket I was wearing. My finger wrapped around the switchblade, then I carefully pulled it out and palmed it. Bella's eyes dropped quickly, and she must have seen what was happening because she started talking.

"Look McMurphy, this doesn't have to get ugly. My girl doesn't know where your wife is. You just let her go and we'll all forget about this."

As the mob boss started droning on about respect and taking things that belonged to him, I took my shot. Pressing my thumb against the button, I released the blade of the knife, then jammed it into the side of McMurphy's thigh as hard as I could.

He howled, loosening his arm, and I dropped to the ground and rolled away. Bella and the bear converged on him at the same time. When I saw McMurphy turn the gun on Bella I leapt up, grabbed the bear spray out of my pocket, and aimed for his face, grateful that I'd taken the time during my confinement to study how the weapons in my pocket worked.

McMurphy dropped the gun, howling in pain as the pepper spray hit his eyes. In a flash, the bear was on him, swiping his great paw across the man's neck and chest. I gasped in shock as he dropped to the ground in a spray of blood, the life leaving his body.

I knew I should be saddened about the loss of a human life, but all I felt was relief. Relief for myself, and most importantly, relief for Robbie and his mother, who wouldn't have to live the rest of their lives hiding and living in fear.

Lois rushed into the room, followed by Wanda, Martha, Angie, and two guys who I assumed were Boris's brothers. They were all in various states of undress, and a couple of them had blood on them, presumably not their own.

There was a roar outside and then another bear came in through the window, one I recognized as Elena. When she reached Boris, she shifted back into a human, totally unconcerned about being naked. That was the thing about shifters, they had no modesty.

"Aw, you killed that abusive asshole crime lord, huh Boris?" she asked, studying the claw marks on McMurphy.

The bear nodded.

"Well, now I have no choice but to take you as my mate," Elena said with a resigned sigh.

Boris the bear roared, then he lifted my naked friend up and threw her over his shoulder, hopping through the window and lumbering away.

"Damned bears, always leaving us with the clean-up," Lois grumbled.

"I'll call a clean-up team, boss," Martha said, picking up her phone.

As everyone sprang into action at once, Bella walked over to me, resting her hands on my shoulders.

"Are you okay, mate?"

"Yeah," I nodded.

"You're not hurt?"

"No."

"Good. Let's go home."

Bella

When we got outside the McMurphy mansion, I took a closer look at Lucy. There was a cut at the side of her mouth and a bruise coming up across her cheek where someone had clearly hit her. My entire body vibrated with rage.

"Who hit you?" I gritted out. "Was it McMurphy or one of his guys?"

If it was one of the henchmen, I was going back inside to break someone's neck. After I eviscerated them. If truth be told, I was disappointed that Boris beat me to McMurphy. After seeing that asshole holding a gun to my mate's head, it should have been me who killed him. I had a feeling that Boris didn't want my mate to see me kill someone though. It might have changed her opinion of me.

Lucy lifted her hand up to cup my cheek. Instinctively I leaned into her touch.

"Look Bella, I'm fine. A little banged up from being tossed around but it's nothing that won't heal in a day or two. But what about you?" she asked. "Last I saw you and the bears, you were all laying in the parking lot with a bunch of poisoned arrows in your body."

"They shot us with shifter strength tranqs, but vamps metabolize faster than shifters. I probably was out twenty minutes or so, and all traces of the poison were gone in an hour or so."

"And Boris and Elena?" she asked. "They looked okay just now, but are they?"

"Yeah, those bears have so much muscle mass they processed it pretty quickly too. Plus they were fueled by righteous indignation. We were all embarrassed to be taken down by a bunch of humans. Now let's get out of here."

I threaded my fingers through my mate's, then led her to one of the SUVs. Once we were in the car and heading down the long private road to the mansion, Lucy said, "I can't believe you guys brought Elena. She's not an operative, you know. She's a kindergarten teacher."

"With you missing and Boris coming along, we couldn't keep her away from here," I explained. "We made her promise to wait outside until it was safe though. I don't know if you realize this, but your friend is kind of stubborn."

"Do you think she and Boris are okay?" Lucy asked.

"Oh yeah, with the way he carried her off, they'll be fucking each other's brains out within the hour, right after he puts his mark on her neck, I promise you that."

"What about us?" she asked. "Will we be fucking each other's brains out within the hour too?"

I damn near drove off the road at her words.

"You're hurt," I hedged.

"And a good orgasm flooding my system with endorphins will do wonders for that," she said. "And rumor has it, you're good at sex. Unless you were exaggerating?"

"I wasn't exaggerating," I growled.

"All right then. Now tell me about this mate thing. How does it all work?"

I paused, gathering my thoughts.

"It works differently depending on who your mate is. For supes, as I told you we recognize our mates right away. Our inner animals or demons as the case may be, they start pushing on us, demanding that we complete the mate bond as soon as possible."

"And how does that happen? Is this the marking Elena referenced?"

"Yeah," I said. "You, um, well you bite your mate, leave a mark on them somewhere, and that activates the bond."

"I assume this isn't just a little nip?" she asked.

"It's a pretty deep bite, but it usually happens during orgasm, and once the mate bond activates you're filled with endorphins so they say it doesn't really hurt."

"I would have thought you needed to drink my blood or something."

For some reason that made me feel a little embarrassed. "Well, we lick the wound to help seal it back up, and in doing that, we ingest some blood."

"If we do that, when we do that, will I turn into a vampire too?" Lucy asked.

I felt a jolt of excitement at her use of the word 'when'.

"No, we aren't really allowed to turn humans into vamps except in extreme cases, like someone is dying and it's the only way to save them. For the most part, new vampires are created by birth, not by turning humans."

"What happens next?"

"Once we bite our mate, and they bite us back if they're also supes, and the mate bond activates, then it becomes biologically impossible for us to be with someone else as long as our mate is alive," I explained. "If they were to break up, the supe is destined to live a lonely and celibate life."

"You're telling me there is no vampire divorce?" she asked in surprise.

"It's the same for all supernatural beings," I confirmed. "It's biologically impossible for us to cheat on our mates or to fall in love with someone else, even if they die before us."

"Wow."

"With supes, we recognize our fated mates so it's not a big deal, we know instinctively that it's safe to make a lifelong commitment, but humans need time to be certain. To fall in love."

"I don't need time," Lucy said decisively.

I braked, sending us both pitching forward, then pulled over to the side of the road so I could look at her. "What?"

"I don't need time. I'm ready for us to be mated."

"You had a big trauma today," I started slowly. "And a head injury. You shouldn't make any major decisions in this state."

"Bella."

"Yeah?"

"Take me home and make me yours. Now."

I couldn't resist leaning forward and pressing my lips against hers. My inner vamp was begging me to take her right here, but I held her back.

"Are you sure?" I asked Lucy, my forehead pressed against hers.

"I'm sure."

I nodded, suddenly too overcome with emotion to talk, then threw the car into drive and pressed the gas pedal down as far as it would go. I needed to get home. Now.

"Where are we?" Lucy asked a few minutes later as I tore into the parking lot of my apartment building.

"My house. It's closer."

Hopping out of the car, I raced around to the passenger side, and just like Boris had done with Elena, I picked Lucy up and threw her over my shoulder.

"Bella! Oh my God! You're going to hurt yourself!" she squealed.

Ignoring her protests, I hurried to my porch, typing in the code to open the entry door and heading right for the bedroom. Once we got there I slid Lucy slowly down my body, wrapped my arms around her waist and pulled her against my body.

The kiss I gave her was long and claiming and when we broke apart, both of us were breathing heavily. Lucy looked a little dazed.

"Kissing you feels so different than what I'm used to," she said softly. "Every time is more intense."

"That's the mate bond," I explained. "Even if I haven't marked you yet, it's still starting to connect us."

I kissed her again, walking her backwards until her legs bumped up against my bed.

"I need you naked," I rasped. "Now."

"You first," she said teasingly.

We both made quick work of removing our clothes and for the first time I got to see Lucy naked. Her body was lush and curvy, all pale white flesh and tiny brown freckles. I loved it.

"Here's what's going to happen," I said. "I'm going to bury my head between your thighs and eat you out until you forget your name."

My mate shook her head, always stubborn.

"I've got a better idea," she said. "Get on your back."

"I'm not used to being ordered around in bed," I said, even as my body shook with excitement at her tone. I didn't know I had a submissive side.

"Too bad. There are very few people in this world who are bossier than kindergarten teachers."

Lucy

I'd never been passive in sexual relationships, but with Bella I had the strongest urge to be more dominant. Judging by the way her pupils narrowed to slits and her fangs appeared, I was pretty sure she liked it.

She hesitated for just a few seconds before she gracefully spread out on the bed. Her body was long and lean and while I'd gotten up close and personal with her cunt that night I made her come, I hadn't seen her breasts before. They were perky and small, a little more than a handful, with sharp red nipples that I couldn't wait to get a taste of.

I spread myself out on top of her, pushing one of my thighs between hers, then took one nipple into my mouth, teasing it with my tongue. When I bit down lightly, Bella made a moaning sound that send wetness flooding through my core.

Shifting, I lined up my thigh with her pussy and started grinding against her while I kissed my way up her chest. When I reached the juncture of her neck and shoulder, I took a hunk of skin into my mouth, biting down enough that I knew I'd leave a mark without breaking the skin. I might not be able to mark her in the shape shifter way, but I was damn well going to leave at least a temporary mark.

I continued rubbing my thigh against her mound as I moved my head up and gave Bella a long, deep kiss. Our tongues dueled, as we both fought for control of the kiss.

"Don't top from the bottom," I teased as I nipped her lower lip. "Let me take care of you."

"We did that last time," she reminded me.

"Not keeping score," I teased.

Then I kissed her again. I shifted slightly, so my weight was mostly on one side and I could move my hand down her body and between her thighs. Bella was slick with moisture, and my fingers slid easily through her folds. As we continued to kiss, I explored every inch of her before sliding one finger inside her opening. Bella's hips popped up as I started pumping in and out.

"Lucy. That feels so good," she whispered, biting her lip.

"Just wait," I promised, adding a second finger.

I started fucking her with my fingers, picking up speed as I slid along her inner walls, looking for the spot that would send her over the edge. When I found it, I rotated my hand to press the heel of my palm against her clitoris, adding pressure to contrast against the pumping of my fingers.

Lowering my head, I bit her again, this time right over a breast. As I sucked Bella's flesh between my teeth she let go, crying my name as she shuddered and shook beneath me with the force of her orgasm. She was so beautiful, eyes closed, mouth open slightly, gasping my name as she chased her release.

When it was all over, she sagged down against the mattress, panting for breath. I looked with satisfaction at the dark red hickey I'd left on her breast.

Bella pushed me to the side and rolled over until she was half laying on me. "I don't want you to run away this time," she said shakily. "But I need a minute."

"We've got all day," I reminded her.

It was hard to believe with everything that had happened already today, but it was only early afternoon. I wondered idly if anyone had notified the principal that Elena and I were both gone – along with our temporary educational assistants. Getting two substitute teachers on such short notice was almost impossible, which meant that the principal and vice principal had probably taken over the two classrooms.

Then I forgot all about school because Bella was kissing me, apparently recovered from her intense orgasm.

She kissed her way slowly down my body, spending time exploring my breasts, circling my belly button, and making her way down the outside of first one leg and then the other. By the time she pressed a soft kiss against my mound, I was shaking with arousal, desperate to come.

"Please," I gasped. "Bella."

"I ought to torture you for a while," she whispered against my flesh. "But I want this too much."

I bent my knees, opening them to the side to create more space for her, and Bella settled between my legs.

"Such a pretty pussy," she whispered before spreading my labia wide and giving me a long lick from the bottom to top of my slit.

I made a choking noise as waves of pleasure filled my body. Then she did it again. And again, until I was completely lost in the sensations. Everything faded from my mind – the kidnapping, who was covering my classroom, whether I'd paid the electric bill yet – all I could think about was the sensation of Bella's tongue lapping at my pussy over and over again until I was shaking beneath her, desperate to come.

When she took my clitoris into her mouth and added suction I let myself go. Wave after wave of pleasure flooded my body and all I could do was ride the waves, sobbing out Bella's name as the powerful orgasm completely took over.

I was still shaking when Bella scooted up my body and ground her wet pussy against my thigh as she gently kissed the base of my neck.

"Are you sure you're ready for this?" she asked softly. "Can I make you mine? Forever?"

I nodded.

"I need the words, Lucy."

“Mark me,” I said, my voice as clear and sure as my mind was. “Make me your mate.”

The words were scarcely out of my mouth when Bella lowered her head and bit into the flesh of my neck. I felt a brief burst of pain but it was quickly replaced by the most intense sensation of euphoria I’d felt in my life. It triggered another orgasm and as Bella rubbed herself against my thigh, she came again as well.

When she finally pulled back, she was in full vamp mode. Red eyes, fangs, dark red lips covered with blood from licking my wound. With a shaking hand I reached up to where she’d marked me, surprised to realize that the wound was already sealing.

And then I felt the mate bond activating. It was like there was another sensation in my head. Not a being exactly, but more like an awareness. I could feel Bella’s emotions as clearly as I felt my own. It felt weird. Not bad, just weird.

Bella reached down to pull the blanket over us, then we cuddled together, sharing a few quick kisses.

"Hey Bella?" I asked sleepily.

"Yeah?"

"Why do you keep an Air Tag in your jacket pocket?"

Bella grimaced. "I kept losing my jacket. Wanda suggested using an Air Tag, I think as a joke, but it turned out to be a life saver in this case."

"I'm glad I grabbed your jacket then."

“It’s been a big day,” she said with a yawn. “Let’s rest for a while.”

“Okay,” I said softly.

Bella woke me up a few hours later with her lips wrapped around my nipple and a hand sliding between my thighs. We didn’t do any talking for the rest of the day. Instead, we made love over and over again until after midnight when we finally passed out from exhaustion.

I woke up with the sunrise and that’s when the doubt started creeping in. I couldn’t help but wonder if I’d just made a big mistake. After all, what did I even know about this person that I’d essentially tied myself to forever? She’d never even told me one personal thing about her or what her life was like outside of Sapphic Security.

Bella was still sleeping when I slipped out of her apartment. Someone from the team had brought over my bag that got dropped during the ambush, so after leaving Bella a note, I used my phone to call an Uber and headed home. It was Tuesday and I needed to get to work. Now that the threat was over, I could get back to my normal routine.

Maybe after a being away from her a while I would have a better idea about what do about Bella.

I was so distracted with thoughts of the woman who'd rocked my world I wasn't paying attention when I entered my apartment. I was halfway across the living room before I saw the man sitting on my couch. He looked vaguely familiar.

He moved to his feet with an easy grace and sent me a smile that was pure malevolence.

"You must be the woman responsible for my brother's untimely death."

BELLA

I knew something was wrong the instant I woke up. First, it was way too early for me to have woken up on my own. Second, I was alone.

Mate!" the voice inside me was screaming loudly. "O*ur mate is in danger!"*

When I closed my eyes and concentrated on the still strengthening mate bond, I could feel it. A strong sensation of fear. Where was Lucy? I made a quick loop of my apartment until I saw the note she'd left for me on the kitchen island.

Bella,

Have to go to work. Thanks for last night. Talk to you soon.

Lucy

Something about the note felt off to me, like it was written by an acquaintance or a one night stand instead of the woman I'd pledged to spend my life with less than twenty-four hours ago. Stopping only to pull on a pair of jeans and my boots, I flew out of my apartment, my vamp pushing me to hurry.

I called Lois on the way, letting her know that something was going down with Lucy, although I didn't know what. After she assured me that she was sending a team immediately and reminded me not to go in alone, I drove like a bat out of hell over to Lucy's apartment. I flew up the stairs, then made myself pause outside the door, listening and assessing, just like I was trained to do.

"My brother and I were very close, you know," a man was talking inside the apartment. "First you took his family from him and then you took his life. That does not make me very happy, Miss Ingram."

Despite the mild tone, I could feel rage vibrating from him.

"Liam drove his family away with his abuse," Lucy corrected, her voice a little shaky. "And it's not my fault he had a run-in with a grizzly bear. That's what happens when you build a house in the forest."

She cried out as the man hit her. My nails lengthened and sharpened until I drew blood in my palms. I glanced at my phone to see the team was one minute out. I wanted nothing more than to break down this door, but I didn't need to go in halfcocked. I needed to be patient so I could save Lucy.

Less than two minutes later Lois crept up the hallway, Martha behind her. I breathed a sigh of relief. Inside, McMurphy was still yammering onto my mate about how she'd ruined everyone's life. These bad guys always loved hearing the sound of their own voices.

"Wanda and Suzanna are at the back door," Lois mouthed. "Angie and the New Recruit are on the balcony."

My boss didn't bother learning people's names until they passed probation. There were two other people who started at the company at the same time as me. She called us New Recruit One, Two, and Three for our first year of employment.

Lois set the countdown timer on her comms, which went to everyone on the team. Watching it count down from five to one felt like it took a lot longer than the five seconds I knew it did.

When the timer hit zero, all hell broke loose as we all flew into action.

Lois howled like the wolf she was and gave the front door a hard kick right near the lock. The door went flying open just as the rest of the team simultaneously burst through the back door and the sliding door to the balcony. McMurphy was surrounded in less than two seconds. Unfortunately, so was Lucy.

"Don't make me kill her," McMurphy yelled, sounding a little crazed.

He wasn't the calm and cool criminal that his brother had been. The man waved his knife by Lucy's face, nicking the corner of her jaw, and that's when I lost it. Letting my vampire take control, I flew across the room, knocked him to the floor, and sank my teeth into his neck, severing his jugular. The blood gurgled from his neck, and he went limp.

Since he was already dead I took a few gulps of fresh blood. It was delicious. Much better than the donated blood I usually drank. That was full of preservatives to make it last in the refrigerator.

"Bella! Quit eating the criminals!" Lois ordered. "Damned vampires."

This from a woman I'd once seen eating a live rabbit she'd snatched while we were on a stakeout in the woods. She tore off its leg while it was still twitching.

I pushed up to standing and gave my boss a sheepish look. "It smelled good and it was really fresh."

My boss rolled her eyes, but I ignored her, going over to Lucy who was pressed up against the wall. I surreptitiously wiped my mouth with my shirt as I went.

"Are you okay, mate?" I asked, pushing a lock of hair behind her ear.

"I thought you weren't supposed to feed off humans," she said.

I couldn't interpret her expression. The emotions coming through the mate bond felt kind of jumbled.

"It's okay if they're freshly dead," I explained, feeling foolish. "We're allowed then. A little anyway. In certain circumstances."

A little crease formed between Lucy's eyebrows. Had I freaked her out?

"Does this guy have any more brothers?" Lucy asked the room. "Sisters? Parents or spry grandparents? Favorite cousins? Will there be anyone else in the McMurphy family coming after me?"

"The parents are long dead," Wanda called, studying her phone where she'd likely pulled up the entire McMurphy family history. "No other siblings. No kids except for the one you saved. Looks like you're in the clear."

Lucy released a long, shuddering breath. "Okay then, I need to get to work."

I looked at my mate like she'd lost her mind. "You can't go to work after that!"

"I can and I will," she said stubbornly. "Our boss will have our asses if Elena and I call out for a second day."

I sensed avoidance through the bond.

"Fine, then I'll go with you."

Lucy slammed her fists on her hips and gave me that stern kindergarten teacher look that always made me hot.

"I don't need a bodyguard anymore. Wanda said there are no more McMurphys left to come after me."

"You do still need an educational assistant though," I reminded her.

"You're not even wearing a bra!"

"I'm sorry I didn't dress up before I came over and save your damned life after you ditched me this morning," I huffed. "What's this really about?"

"Nothing." She turned on her heel and flounced away. "I'm going to take a shower and get ready for work. I'll let you all deal with the dead body. Feel free to throw away that area rug, I'll never get the blood out of it anyway."

I stared after her, ignoring the snickers and curious looks from my coworkers.

"Boss, I need to take the day off," I told Lois.

"Have fun at kindergarten," she said. "But your ass better be in the office tomorrow. You know how much paperwork we have to do when one of you idiots kills someone."

I resisted pointing out that Lois wouldn't hesitate to kill anyone who so much as gave her mate a threatening look. Instead I asked the team to tell Lucy I'd meet her at school, then I headed home to shower and change into something kindergarten appropriate. And a bra.

When I pulled into the school parking lot I ran into Boris and Elena. The two bears were looking cozy, holding hands and smiling like saps.

"I guess it's official then?" I asked as I caught up with them.

"Yes. Elena is now official mate. I will move into her den, and we will make cubs now," Boris said proudly.

Elena gave him a pointed look. "I told you that if things go okay and you don't annoy me too much, I would *consider* having cubs after we've been together for at least a year."

"You will not want to wait that long," he said confidently.

"Don't bet on it, bear."

I shook my head at their antics. "If you two are done arguing, let me tell you what happened this morning..."

Lucy

My classroom door opened a few minutes before the bell rang. I didn't need to look up to know it was Bella. Even before she'd bit me I'd been able to sense when she was around. The sensation was only stronger now.

"Hey, I thought I'd help today since you don't have a new educational assistant yet."

Bella's voice was soft and oddly tentative. I looked up, then burst out laughing.

"Are you wearing an Oscar the Grouch tee shirt?" I asked incredulously. I'd never seen her wear anything that wasn't plain black.

The shirt was light grey with a picture of Oscar in his trash can. She'd paired the shirt with olive camouflage pants and her black boots. Plus her black leather jacket, of course. I'd given it back to her yesterday.

"My sister gave this shirt to me for Christmas last year," she said defensively. "She said the shirt reminded her of me."

When I didn't say anything she added, "Because I tend to be grumpy."

"Oh, I understand that," I teased. "I didn't even know you had a sister."

Bella walked closer. "The thing about the supernatural world is that we tend to mate first and get to know each other after. Getting together is basically a foregone conclusion, so we figure we've got our whole lives to get to know each other. But I understand that's the opposite of the human world."

I nodded. "Yeah, if I tell my parents we're shifter married after knowing each other for only a week they will stroke out."

"Well how about this?" she asked. "Now that everything has settled down, let's take some time to get to know each other better."

"Can we still have sex?" I asked.

"Goddess, I hope so," she replied fervently, making me laugh.

The bell rang, telling me the kids would be here in less than a minute.

"Are you free for dinner tonight?" I asked. "Or will you still be full from eating McMurphy?"

For some reason, seeing Bella drinking blood from a dying man's neck hadn't grossed me out as much as it probably should have.

Bella smirked. "I think I'll be hungry by then," she said.

"Okay, then we're going on a date, like normal people," I said. "We have some catching up to do. We'll do it over pasta and wine."

My morning classes flew by. Boris and Elena came to join us for lunch and the four of us discussed the confrontations with both of the McMurphy brothers and associated rescue operations.

"What happens now?" I asked Elena when Boris and Bella went to take playground duty, leaving us alone. "Are you and Boris a couple now?"

Elena bit her lip. "Yeah. Now he wants to move in with me, and I said that I'd consider it, but I'm putting him off for a while. Things are moving kind of fast."

"I thought you shifters liked fast?" I asked.

"I'm not your average shifter," my friend replied. "I may have let Boris mark me, and I marked him back in the heat of the moment, but that doesn't mean I'm going to turn into some trad bear."

"Trad bear?" I asked in confusion.

"The bear version of trad wives," she explained. "I don't want to live like some traditional homemaker, focused only on keeping the house, cooking, and raising kids. I want to keep my career and my friends."

"Well Boris has the restaurant and his contract security work, it seems like you can both have separate lives in addition to your life together."

"What about you and Bella?" she asked. "I might say the same to you. I can't help but notice that mark on your neck, you little slut."

I rolled my eyes at her teasing. "We're mated but we're going to date for a while. See how that goes."

Elena laughed. "The only question is which one of us caves first. I have a bad feeling that neither of us will last a month before moving our mates in, despite our best intentions."

My friend wasn't wrong. Boris moved in with her two weeks later, after a long negotiation about roles and independence that Elena insisted that they put in writing. Her mate agreed of course. He was so smitten with Elena he would do anything she asked, anyone with eyes could see that.

As for me and Bella, we made it about a month before I finally came around to the idea that we could move in together. But before I told her, I wanted her to meet my parents. That's how one Sunday we made our way to the suburbs for Sunday dinner.

Bella's mouth dropped open as we drove up to the house in Lake Washington and parked by the five car garage.

"Holy crap, I had no idea you were rich!"

"My parents are rich," I corrected. "I'm just a kindergarten teacher."

She leaned across the console to give me a quick kiss. "You're the most beautiful and talented kindergarten teacher ever," she said loyally.

I rolled my eyes but still felt warm. "Yeah okay, you already got me. Let's go meet my parents."

To my relief, my parents took to Bella immediately. The fact that she'd helped save my life went a long way with them of course, but they were also thrilled that I was serious about someone.

"Lucy never brought anyone home before," my mother told her. "Not even back when she was dating boys."

Bella raised one eyebrow and sent me an amused look. "You dated boys?"

"Only in high school."

For his part my father bonded with her over their shared love of the military. Like Bella, Dad had spent several years in the Army, and he peppered her with questions about her tours and the things she'd seen and done while she was in the service.

After we shared a very pleasant dinner, my mother professed her approval.

"I love Bella for you," she told me as we loaded the dishwasher.

I looked over my shoulder to make sure we were alone before whispering, "Bella is a vampire."

Mom nodded. "Yes dear, your father told me she was supernatural. I would have guessed vampire based on how pale she is, and her energy is different than the shifters we know," she explained. "We're not biased, don't worry. If Bella makes you happy, then we're happy with Bella."

And that was that. Bella had my parents' approval, we were officially mated, and after spending the last month talking and getting to know everything about each other, it was time for the next step.

"I'm ready for us to move in together," I told Bella as soon as we walked in the front door of my apartment.

She stilled, then looked at me over her shoulder cautiously. "You are?"

I nodded. "Yes."

Bella walked back, crowding me against the door with her palms on either side of my head.

"There's just one thing," I continued. "Well, maybe two things."

Bella lowered her head to nuzzle my neck. "What?"

"I don't really like either of our apartments," I said. "I want to find a better place. Some place with a lot of natural light for my plants."

"There's a house for sale up the street from Boris and Elena," she said. "Boris told me about it yesterday."

"I don't know if I can afford to buy a house," I said regretfully.

"I have a lot of money saved up," Bella said, moving to nip at the shell of my ear. "I can do the downpayment as a wedding present."

"A wedding present?" I gasped.

"I assumed you wanted to make things official in the human world?" she asked. "Plus we'll save money on our taxes."

"Wow, that was romantic," I teased.

She grabbed my hips and boosted me up against the door, shoving one muscled thigh between my legs.

"You want romantic, you're with the wrong woman," she said, sliding me up and down her thigh. I gasped at the delicious friction. "How about I make it up to you by making you come your brains out?"

"I wouldn't object to that," I said breathlessly.

Bella gave me a long, claiming kiss, one hand cupping and squeezing my breast while the other held onto my hip. I wrapped my legs around her hips and arched my back against the door, using that as leverage so I could drag my pussy against her thigh. I was still wearing my panties and with every roll of my hips the fabric dragged across my sensitive pussy.

"Fuck," I dropped my head against the door, gasping for breath. "I'm close."

Somehow every time we made love it was even hotter than the last time.

"Let go, mate," Bella growled.

She lowered her head, sealing her lips over the spot where she'd marked me the night after I was kidnapped. She didn't break the skin, but just the touch of her teeth and the addition of suction made the mate mark burn and throb, the pain turning to a pleasure that sent me right over the edge.

Fire raced down my spine and then I was flying, my eyes squeezed closed as I rode the waves of my pleasure. Through it all, Bella continued to drag me over her thigh, keeping the friction going until I finally sagged against the door, totally spent.

Gently she lowered my feet to the ground, then pressed a kiss to my forehead.

"You look so beautiful when you come, mate."

I wrapped my arms around her and pulled Bella into a long hug while I caught my breath.

"What's the second thing?" she asked.

"Huh?"

"Earlier, you said there were two things you needed for us to move in together."

I laughed. "The second thing I was going to tell you was that I wanted to get married, but you beat me to it. I love you and want to make things official in both worlds."

"I love you too, mate," Bella said. "I can't wait to make you mine. Again."

Epilogue—Bella

Four years later…

A high-pitched scream broke the quiet of the summer day, making Elena sigh heavily.

"You get them," she said to Boris. "You're the one that insisted on knocking me up."

"Of course my love."

Lucy and I exchanged an amused look as Boris lumbered off after his twin sons. They were almost three years old and already a handful. But despite Elena's earlier fears, Boris had proved himself to be an involved and attentive parent. He told me once that he was determined to be the father that he never had. His brothers also did a lot, taking their role as uncles very seriously.

The baby that was strapped to my chest started crying and I rocked back and forth gently, rocking little Lanie back to sleep. We'd named her after Elena but then the twins started calling her Lanie and it stuck.

She was a good baby, already sleeping through the night, and as much as I loved my job at Sapphic Security, I was a little sad that my four month family leave was going to be over in a week. At least Lucy was off school for two more months. It was going to kill both of us when we had to put little Lanie in daycare.

The past four years had flown by. Not long after we made our second commitment Lucy's parents had thrown us a wedding. It was larger and more elaborate than either of us wanted, but we didn't protest, mostly because it was so important to Lucy's mother. I got along great with her parents, which was nice since my own parents had passed away years ago. I loved being part of a family again.

We'd purchased the house a couple doors down from Boris and Elena's and we spent a ton of time at each other's houses, having barbecues and game nights, watching sports, and playing with the kids. We frequently had our coworkers over with their families too. It was nice. Way more domestic than I'd ever expected.

Meanwhile my sister Darla had been discharged from the Army and moved to Seattle to live close to us. Lois hired her at Sapphic Security as soon as she got here, but hadn't bothered to learn her name until she knew Darla would work out as a security agent.

Darla had recently found her mate – on the job of course – and was trying to work through some issues to get the super smart human doctor to accept her.

Lucy and I waited a while before deciding to have a baby. Neither of us was completely sure at first that we wanted to be parents, but after spending time with Boris and Elena's twins we decided it was the right decision for us. Lucy's parents had been over the moon when we told them.

It took a couple of rounds of treatment before Lucy got pregnant, but she made pregnancy look easy, and despite the fact that Lanie was only four months old, we were already thinking about having a second baby next year.

Boris came back with a kid on each hip, handing one to Elena before sitting down again. Whatever he'd said to the kids, they were suddenly quiet.

"We have news that is very big," Boris said. "We are having more cubs."

"Freaking twins again," Elena groaned. "This asshole knocked me up with two more giant bear babies, like the first two didn't almost kill me."

"Is not my fault twins run in family," he replied, leaning over to press a kiss to her cheek. "Your mate is how you say? Stud."

Despite his years here, he still had a pretty thick accent, especially when he was excited about something.

We all burst out laughing, even Elena. Despite the constant bickering between the two bears, they were obviously very much in love. And great parents.

"Congratulations!" Lucy sprang out of her chair to give them each a hug. "I'm so happy for you guys."

"I was wondering when you were going to tell us," I added. "I smelt that you were pregnant weeks ago."

Lucy smacked my shoulder. "Why didn't you tell me?"

"I didn't want to ruin the surprise," I replied.

"We have good life here," Boris said, his voice thick with satisfaction.

The only thing that bothered him was that neither Yuri nor Alexei had found their own mates yet, despite everyone we knew doing their best to fix them up.

I put my arm around my mate, and she lowered her head to press a quick kiss to our sleeping daughter's forehead.

"We really do have a good life. I'm glad we found each other, even if we had to deal with the mob for it to happen."

"From sorrow comes joy," Boris intoned. It was pretty optimistic for the Belarusian.

"That it does," I said, squeezing Lucy's shoulders. "That it does."

***

If you liked this book, please consider leaving a review or rating to let me know.

You can find more of Reba's lesbian romances at *Books2read.com/rl/lesbianromance*

Be sure to join my newsletter for more great books. You'll receive a free book when you join my newsletter. Subscribers are the first to hear about all of my new releases and sales. Visit my mailing list sign-up at https://bit.ly/RebaBaleSapphic to download your free book today.

Keep reading for a preview of another Reba Bale sapphic romance.

Special Preview of The Divorcee's First Time

A Contemporary Lesbian Romance by Reba Bale

"It's done," I said triumphantly. "My divorce is final."

My best friend Susan paused in the process of sliding into the restaurant booth, her sharply manicured eyebrows raising almost to her hairline. "Dickhead finally signed the papers?" she asked, her tone hopeful.

I nodded as Susan settled into the seat across from me. "The judge signed off on it today. Apparently his barely legal girlfriend is knocked up, and she wants to get a ring on her finger before the big event." I explained with a touch of irony in my voice. "The child bride finally got it done for me."

Susan smiled and nodded. "Well congratulations and good riddance. Let's order some wine."

We were most of the way through our second bottle when the conversation turned back to my ex. "I wonder if Dick-head and his Child Bride will last for the long haul," Susan mused.

I shook my head and blew a chunk of hair away from my mouth.

"I doubt it," I told her. "Someday she's gonna roll over and think, there's got to be something better out there than a self-absorbed man child who doesn't know a clitoris from a doorknob."

Susan laughed, sputtering her wine. I eyed her across the table. Although she was ten years older than me, we had been best friends for the last five years. We worked together at the accounting firm. She had been my trainer when I first came there, fresh out of school with my degree. We bonded over work, but soon realized that we were kindred spirits.

Susan was rapidly approaching forty but could easily pass for my age. Her hair was black and shiny, hinting at her Puerto Rican heritage, with blunt bangs and blond highlights that she paid a fortune for. Her face was clear and unlined, with large brown eyes and cheek bones that could cut glass. She was an avid runner and worked hard to maintain a slim physique since the women in her family ran towards the chunkier side.

I was almost her complete opposite. Blonde curls to her straight dark hair, blue eyes instead of brown, curvy where she was lean, introverted to her extrovert.

But somehow, we clicked. We were closer than sisters. Honestly, I don't know how I would have gotten through the last year without her. She had been the first one I called when my marriage fell apart, and she had supported me throughout the whole process.

It had been a big shock when I came home early one day and found my husband getting a blow job in the middle of our living room. It had been even more shocking when I saw the fresh young face at the other end of that blow job.

"What the fuck are you doing?" I had screeched, startling them both out of their sex stupor. "You're getting blow jobs from children now?"

The girl had looked up from her knees with eyes glowing in righteous indignation. "I'm not a child, I'm nineteen," she had informed me proudly. "I'm glad you finally found out. I give him what you don't, and he loves me."

I looked into the familiar eyes of my husband and saw the panic and confusion there. I made it easy for him. "Get out," I told him firmly, my voice leaving no room for argument. "Take your teenage girlfriend and get the fuck out. We're getting a divorce. Expect to hear from my lawyer."

The condo was in my name. I had purchased it before we were married, and since I had never added his name to the deed, he had no rights to it. There was no question he would be the one leaving.

My husband just stared at me with his jaw hanging open like he couldn't believe it. "But Jennifer," he whined. "You don't understand. Let me explain."

"There's nothing to understand," I told him sadly. "This is a deal breaker for me, and you know that as well as I do. We are done."

The girl had taken his hand and smiled triumphantly. "Come on baby," she told him. "Zip up and let's get out of here. We can finally be together like we planned."

"Yeah baby," I had sneered. "I'll box up your stuff. It'll be in the hallway tomorrow. Pick it up by six o'clock or I'm trashing it all."

After they left my first call was to the locksmith, but my second call was to Susan.

That night was the last time I had seen my husband until we had met for the court-ordered pre-divorce mediation. He spent most of that session reiterating what he had told me in numerous voice mails, emails and sessions spent yelling on the other side of my front door. He loved me. He had made a terrible mistake. He wasn't going to sign the papers. We were meant to be together. Needless to say, mediation hadn't been very successful. Fortunately, I had been careful to keep our assets separate, as if I knew that someday I would be in this situation.

Through it all, Susan had been my rock. In the end I don't think I was even that sad about the divorce, I was really angrier with myself for staying in a relationship that wasn't fulfilling with a man I didn't love anymore.

"You need to get some quality sex." Susan drew my attention back to the present. "Bang him out of your system."

"I don't know," I answered slowly. "I think I need a hiatus."

"A hiatus from what?" Susan asked with a frown. "You haven't had sex in what, eighteen months?"

I nodded. "Yeah, but I just can't take a disappointing fumble right now. I would rather have nothing than another three-pump chump."

I shook my head and continued, "I'm going to stick with my battery-operated boyfriend, he never disappoints me."

Susan smiled. "That's because you know your way around your own vajayjay."

She motioned to the waiter to bring us a third bottle of wine.

"That's why I like to date women," she continued. "We already know our way around the equipment."

I nodded thoughtfully. "You make a good point."

Susan leaned forward. "We've never talked about this," she said earnestly. "Have you ever been with a woman?"

For more of the story, check out "The Divorcee's First Time" by Reba Bale, available for immediate download at https://books2read.com/Divorcee.

***

Want a free book? Join my newsletter and a special gift. I'll contact you a few times a month with story updates, new releases, and special sales. Visit https://books.rebabale.com/lesbianromance for more information.

Other Books by Reba Bale

Check out my other books, available on most major online retailers now. Go to at https://rebabale.com/ to learn more.

Friends to Lovers Lesbian Romance Series

The Divorcee's First Time

My BFF's Sister

My Rockstar Assistant

My College Crush

My Fake Girlfriend

My Secret Crush

My Holiday Love

My Valentine's Gift

My Spring Fling

My Forbidden Love

My Office Wife

My Second Chance

Coming Out in Ten Dates

Worth Waiting For

My Party Planner

My Broken Heart

My New Teacher

My New Year

My Big Secret

My Last Chance

The Surrender Club Lesbian Romance Series

Jaded

Hated

Fated

Saved

Caged

Dared

Stuck with You

The Sapphic Security Series

Guarding the Senator's Daughter

Guarding the Rock Star

Guarding the Witness

Guarding the Billionaire

Guarding the Teacher

Guarding the Doctor

Playing to Win Lesbian Sports Series

Tumbling for Love

Racing for Love

Spiking for Love

The Second Chances Lesbian Romance Series

The Woman Before

Last Christmas

The Summer I Fell in Love

Snowed in With You

My Kind of Girl

Kiss Me Softly

Menage Romances

Pie Promises

Tornado Warning

Summer in Paradise

Life of the Mardi

Bases Loaded

Two for One Deal

Penalty Box

Rock My Heart

The Unexpectedly Mine Series

Sinful Desires

Taken by Surprise

Just One Night

Forbidden Desires

Spanking & Sprinkles

Hotwife Erotic Romances

Hotwife in the Woods

Hotwife on the Beach

Hotwife Under the Tree

A Hotwife's Retreat

Hot Wife Happy Life

Want a free book? Just join my newsletter at https://books.rebabale.com/lesbianromance. ***You'll be the first to hear about new releases, special sales, and free offers.***

About Reba Bale

Reba Bale writes erotic romance, lesbian romance, menage romance, & the spicy stories you want to read on a cold winter's night.

She lives in the Northwest with her family and two very spoiled dogs. When Reba is not writing she is reading the same naughty stories she likes to write.

For all of Reba's stories visit her webpage at https://books2read.com/rebabale.

You can hear all about new releases and special sales by joining Reba's mailing list at ***https://books.rebabale.com/lesbianromance***.

Printed in Dunstable, United Kingdom

65374302R00131